BOOK TWELVE OF THE
RIM CONFEDERACY

Captured
Aliens

by Jim Rudnick

 RUDNICK PRESS

ISBN-13: 978-1-988144-26-9
Copyright © 2016
Jim Rudnick

 RUDNICK PRESS

For my Susan...

The RIM Confederacy: Captured Aliens

"While Duke Tanner Scott takes over the reins of the Duchy, there are other forces at work that will challenge his new role. The alien Praix suddenly show up off Ghayth to begin to take over the RIM Confederacy and the Issians appear to not be able to help. Add to his woes as his sister charged with the two murders at his wedding goes to trial for murder and that his protege declares his love for her too.

Meanwhile the Leudies offer to help the upcoming battle with the Praix by lending their new Power Belts to the RIM Task Force and that is matched by the offer of the Caliph to lend his Xithricite clad ships as well. Even the Baroness knows that these aliens are a superior race and their technology is something to be feared as she pushes her navy to come up with a plan.

Added to all of this, is the sudden find of more Praix technology on the wreck on Ghayth. And the secretive move by the Praix as they are attacked by surprise by a rogue Barony navy captain means that once again, on the RIM, lines are drawn in the sand."

A Message to you from the Author...

I just wanted to say thanks so so much for reading Book Eleven of the RIM Confederacy!

As my Amazon bio says, being a youngster in the 1950's meant that I was a voracious reader in what has been called the Golden Age of Science Fiction. That meant that for me, my heroes were not on the hockey rink or gridiron - but instead in my local Library where at 12 I had a full Adult card (thanks Dad!) and took out more than 5 books a week.

Everyone from Heinlein, Norton, Leiber, Pohl, Anderson, Simak, Asimov, Brackett, Gunn, Van Vogt and more....I fell in love with and eventually owned Ace Doubles of my own. And while I never knew who wrote the Tom Corbett - Space Cadet series, I fell in love with them and they had a place of honor on my own bookcase too!

With that kind of an introduction to Science Fiction, it's no wonder that when I got my writing work done, I turned my own fictional side of my brain to writing same. It's one thing I know how to write - and a totally different matter to release same to the world - something that I've just started to work on....

Suffice it to say my own works are rooted in that Golden Age and it's that era that I'd like to one day be known as a teensy contributor to in some small way...

So once again, thanks for beginning my RIM Confederacy series and wait'll you learn about the alcoholic spaceship captain that is my hero, who fights and beats aliens but not the bottle!

Enjoy and remember, in a series, characters develop and mature not the way we sometimes want...instead, it's like they have a life of their own!

And while you can read the series in any order, I'd highly recommend to start with Pirates, then Sleeper Ship, Prison Planet, Ancient Relics, Hospital Ship, Desert Planet, Ruined Memories, Eons Semester, Trade Wars, Brothers Pride, Honeymoon Bottle and Captured Aliens too...and yes, there's more coming soon too!

Prologue ~

The Praix had been in a hurry, suffering from technology issues, yet they still made the seventy-nine thousand lights in less than an hour. That was the first leg into this new galaxy, and it was to be followed by more than a hundred more lights, as the ship tried to hide its real destination by using both inward and outward milk-run locations in the Milky Way. It took more than four days to travel, double back, jump again, then back again, and finally inward and then outward, as it hid its real goal.

Copper plates at the back end of their huge craft almost glowed as they repelled away from the hastily jury-rigged satellite that they'd set up only a day ago. The Engineering Flock had handled it, and they swore that it would work. Not as quickly as the satellite that had been destroyed months ago on their home world, but it would get the Praix ship, the *Wisp*, to its destination.

As it took a path away from its home world, behind it, their home lay in waste and ruin.

As the central core cluster of the SagD Galaxy, the Class III cluster had been more than the head of civilization for that small galaxy. It had taken more than fifty millennia for the Praix to rise from the branches of their home world trees to becoming the most powerful sentient race in SagD Galaxy.

They had settled on planets in the surrounding local group of galaxies spread out over almost five million lights. There were now dozens of thousands of Praix colonies, and here in SagD, they were being destroyed.

From where the invaders of SagD had come, no one knew; not a single beak had been able to define where they had come from. But come they had. These invaders did not communicate. They asked for nothing. They simply appeared in a system and eradicated any ships they found. And moved on. And took nothing.

With more than ten thousand worlds in SagD being settled and colonies opening up still every year, the Praix had prided themselves on their ability to be a sane and civilized master race. Yes, some small factions had troubles being assimilated by the Praix, but with their superior technology, all had fallen before them. Some had been eradicated. Others offered slavery to remain alive at least. But all had fallen before the Praix.

Conquerors seldom faced new forces that could withstand them—or defeat them. And from what the Praix had seen, these invaders were simply eradicating anything they found. Everything they found. The appearance of this new unknown race with their smaller faster ships had been a surprise.

The Praix had fallen at each encounter. The new invaders had sent out a beam that destroyed their ships. Their planets had been simply burned up as the invaders dropped a bomb into their sun, and the resulting nova had ended all life within the Cinderella zone.

The invaders moved like a black curtain across SagD — destroying ships and putting out suns.

This was an invasion that had never been countenanced before ... the death of an empire — at least in SagD.

So the Praix had run.

Huge freighter ships were converted into refugee ships, carrying them away to other galaxies where safety might lie. From the large and small Magellanic clouds, Bootes, Ursa Major, Fornax, and Andromeda too — all had been sent ships, and tens of thousands of ships had fled SagD.

There was no other way to look at it, and this ship, the *Wisp*, had been well down the list when it came to safe havens to run to. As there were few other locations, the *Wisp* had been sent into the vast Milky Way Galaxy to a location where the Praix had once considered for colonization in this galaxy — Ghayth.

The Ghayth colonization experiment had gone awry when the enormous freighter ship had crashed onto the planet itself, and their slaves had been deposited onto Eons. They'd not been back in twenty millennia, but the recent Ansible notation from Ghayth spoke of the ability of someone there to be able to be brought into the Praix fold.

At least that's what the crew on the *Wisp* thought, and they all perched, waiting to drop out of subspace and into orbit around the planet.

CHAPTER ONE

As he turned away from the console, Tanner sighed, and across the small sitting room, Helena grunted loudly.

"My darling," he said contritely, "is there a problem—one that this husband cannot see at all?" he asked.

While he waited for a reply, she toyed with the ends of her beautiful blonde hair. *I love the color of her hair,* Tanner thought, *it's the color of honey and those ash tree leaves in the fall on ... on ... what the hell is the name of that planet?* Her pink onesie made her look a bit like a Garnuthian rabbit—all soft and cuddly.

She looked up at him, her tablet in her lap as she sat draped on the comfortable loveseat across from the desk where he was working. The grin on her face spoke more to him of testing than teasing. She eyed him and then clicked the tablet a couple of times, and something he couldn't see came up.

"Ready?" she asked, and he nodded in response.

"Name of the third planet to join the Duchy d'Avigdor, year and duke of same?" she inquired as she looked down at the answers on the screen that he still couldn't see.

"Um ..." Tanner said, "that would be Dover— joined the duchy almost two hundred years ago under Duke Samuel d'Avigdor. Right?" he asked, and she smiled a smile that said yes.

"Planet with almost no native economy yet enjoys one of the highest per capita incomes?" she replied.

"Anulet, due to it being kept as a native ecology sanctuary. Hunting is the real reason the planet does so well," he said as he unconsciously rubbed his right leg. He recalled being caught by a Jael, the biggest carnivore on Anulet and almost being the animal's dinner, which had been a close call. Time spent in a robo-doc, followed by the lifelong friendship of Duke David d'Avigdor had been the result of his only trip to Anulet.

Tanner smiled and continued. "The tourist economy there is outstanding, and it grows as there are more and more 'neo-ecology' buffs coming in monthly." "This must be a growing concern here on the RIM as well as inwards. We keep Anulet pure

—yes, there is hunting allowed but all controlled and licensed by us. Yes, there are many continents with tours—water-rafting tours, waterfall tours, hiking the huge sub-arctic canyon tours, canoe and kayak tours ... the list is long, but keeping Anulet pure is a good thing."

Helena nodded once again. "And what about Waterloo," she asked.

He drew a blank. Waterloo, he did remember, had joined the Duchy d'Avigdor almost seventy years ago. The planet was based on the economy of its large mineral deposits, and that meant that it was heavily industrialized as far as mining went. But all of its raw materials—ores and precious metals and rare earths were sent off planet for processing.

He fumbled that answer and realized it as he paused to try to find more in his gray matter to help boost his answer up to being current and correct. He had nothing else, he realized, and he shook his head.

"You added just the past weekend," Helena said as she turned off the tablet in her lap and took a drink of the Quaran Syrah they were sharing, "that you thought there was a great possibility to help Waterloo—by adding in refining and smelting industry too. At least that's what you said—not that I know what might even be needed to do that kind of world building," she finished off and emptied her glass too.

Tanner got up, went around the desk, and plopped on the loveseat beside her, carrying the rest of the bottle to share with her. He smiled at his wife and swept a long blonde lock away from her face as he poured. "One thing is for sure. Knowing as much about your realm as you can learn—pound into your brain—is a good way to be a better Royal. Just wish that David had left me a 'Blood of the Duchy d'Avigdor' book like you Barony Royals have," he said.

She nodded. "Maybe there is one, but with David leaving us so soon, perhaps he'd just not yet gotten around to leaving its location available for whomever was to follow."

They were talking about the book, which existed, as far as they knew, only for the Barony. It held the knowledge of the current Baron—or Baroness—written and then passed down from generation to generation. That book had triggered his quest to go to Ghayth on a test drive of the then newest Barony ship—the *Atlas*—on its shakedown cruise. The book held more, much, much more, and its hidden pages lay now in the duke's office here as it belonged to Helena. It might have instead gone to the current Baroness, but Helena's father, the baron, had given it instead to her—with the caution that it was never

14

to go to his wife.

"If there were such a book, surely he'd have left some information about it on the chance that he might not get the opportunity in the future. At least I would think so ..." Tanner said, sipping the supple wine as he talked.

"And you, Mister Duke? Where did you leave that hint for whomever will follow you," she asked with a hint of irony.

He grinned at her. "Everyone knows that wives outlive their husbands—and you know it's in my office in the wall safe behind the huge hologram of the RIM Confederacy. And you have the combination too—we must thank Ambassador Bedre for that. Hey, maybe we should change that?" he asked.

She nodded and said, "Sure, have the AI change it to something you and I would know—and no one else?"

He grinned at her still. "How about how many times we made love that first night on the *Sterling*?" he said.

She laughed. "While it was a glorious pleasure," she said, shaking a finger at him, "it is also not a big enough number for a combination number."

He nodded and looked over at the far table where another bottle of wine stood, open and breathing but still twenty feet away.

15

He sighed, went over to retrieve same, and returned in a second or two. As he refreshed their glasses, he looked out the close side of the room's window and saw the moon over Neen was rising on the horizon.

As the moon rose, it bathed the palace grounds between him and the horizon with an amber color that was so pretty, he snorted, and when Helena cocked her head at him, he held out his hand.

The two went to the window, perched a hip on the edge of the bookcase there, and looked out at the duchy around them.

They saw gardens, ponds, and a row of trees with that great double grain and red and white color from another planet. *Those trees are from ... from ... oh, hell, I have no idea,* he thought. There were hedges that grew in a maze off to one side, and while they rose up only about nine feet, they were so much fun, Ambassador Bedre had said on his guided tour of the palace, for the children of the duchy who came every spring for the big festival.

On the far right side, he could see the palace festival grounds where, years earlier, he had been the guest of honor after saving the duke's life. Here he had seen the Bacu and their busking skills, the log rolling contests and their superior lumberjacks from Anulet, and the choirs from Alto; he had also had his first real meeting with the Master Adept.

She'd warned him about his future and that it lay "in her hands." No mention of who those hands belonged to, and he'd thought, as had Bram, that Helena might be the one. It had turned out to be the Baroness, but still, now in retrospect, Helena looked after his future. Sort of. He tossed off the rest of his glass in one big swig.

"About the prettiest I think I've ever seen," he said and he meant it.

Helena squeezed his hand and smiled up at him.

"As far as I'm concerned, there's only one other palace that is in the running ... perhaps one day we can compare," she said, and they both nodded as the moon rose over the Duchy d'Avigdor.

Professor Scholes knew what she'd just read was important. The weekly report from Reynolds, the xeno team leader on the wrecked alien ship on Ghayth, was very important.

"Might even say," she said to herself, "that it might mean that one of the team, Ellen, could be the ticket into getting the wreck back up and fully powered. Or maybe not. Only testing would tell, and that would come later."

But for now, she had to send off an encrypted Ansible to the Caliph. The Caliph. Her lover. One day to be the most important head of state on the

RIM.

And while she'd never sit beside him, she was his mistress, and that alone was important enough to make her his mole. She was his eyes and ears on the Ghayth wreck, and this was another opportunity to help him gain information about the aliens.

Ellen had somehow been able to get her DNA into the wrecked ship's database and had been recognized as being a crewmember. Ellen was now a crewmember who could simply touch a device or a console screen, and it would power up and accept her commands.

There had been some issues with testing, she remembered. Professor Beedles, the xeno team member in charge of artifacts, had worked all this out—at least at the start when Ellen had been playing with the 'alien ladder' as it was now called. The alien ladder was simple plates and perch bars, but when Ellen had first picked the plate up, it had given her a shock. She'd dropped the plate, but when she picked it up again, it suddenly had a display that she could see. Placing the perch bar over that plate had created an anti-grav situation. Upon seeing it, Beedles had said it would work for the aliens just like a ladder worked for humans— hence the name had stuck.

The testing had begun then, and so far, Ellen the xeno team customs and society professor, had been the guinea pig for just about everything on board the wreck. Cheryl remembered how Ellen would grumble about being dragged away from the study of icons on what they thought might have been the wall of a perch room or bedroom to walk thousands of feet down the wreck's hulk, just to put her hand on a new plate recently found or uncovered. Mostly, nothing happened. But sometimes the plate chimed—not a human-sounding chime but more of a chirp-sounding chime—and then something else happened.

They had learned the chime didn't mean that whatever was happening was within sight or even close them. Once in a while, they could see the changes that Ellen's system-identified hand brought, but other times, they had no clue what happened.

Still, tomorrow, they were going to test Ellen on the bridge, Reynolds, the xeno team leader, had said, and that would be of interest, Cheryl thought, to the Caliph.

Applying human knowledge, the bridge was where everything that was anything on a ship originated, and the xeno team members believed this would hold true for the wreck. Since the bridge was where the ship itself was controlled, bringing in a pseudo-crewmember would be a good thing, she reasoned. "Hope so, at least as long as nothing goes horribly wrong," she said to herself, and then she remembered at the post-dinner briefing, Major Stal had said there was an extra duty shift of marines inbound in case something occurred.

Eating in a tent and sleeping in quarters on a spaceship was all new to her, but Cheryl realized she was living and breathing changes—big changes —that were coming to the RIM Confederacy.

She breathed quietly to herself, counting off ten deep breaths. She sat at the console at her side desk with both feet propped up on her bunk. She had already turned the whole view-screen into a display of the night sky above Ghayth and she could see some stars at least. The changes to the planet and its weather, being worked on by the best climatologists that could be found in the Barony, were starting to take hold as their foray into ocean temperature began to work.

Strengthening tropical winds pushed warmer air from the huge oceans to the west onto the southern continent, and the warmer air carried much less precipitation than had been the case now for centuries. Drier conditions were already making small changes to the coastal mountain range. Here, well inland, and on the southern beaches of the southern continent, the changes were focused even more.

It hadn't rained now in three days. *Not that it*

might not tomorrow, Cheryl thought, but the climatologists were just getting used to working on a global scale, and that meant the changes were probably polarized at this point. She thought small changes were the way to go, but she didn't know for sure; the science behind climate change was beyond her, and if not for the monthly briefing, she'd be in the dark.

Still, no rain every single day was a delightful change.

She looked over at the view-screen, decided the stars would have to wait, and turned back to her business at hand.

She opened the xeno team leader's report on-screen and captured a print screen of the report. She opened a simple image viewer to view the captured report image and saved the picture of the report, still fully readable, as an image. She attached the image file to an email with the subject line of "hi" and then hit the ENCRYPT button on the console in her shipboard quarters. Moments later, her encrypted email was ready to send. She hit SEND and off it went to Neres University to her teaching assistant for the course on Ancient Roorian dialects. He was charged with the simple task to forward it to a disposable email address at Gallipedia, where an aide to the Caliph would retrieve it.

Convoluted, yes, but it would hide her tracks, and she knew that this had to be done.

No one—specifically, no one on the xeno team or in the Barony—knew she was mistress to the Caliph and as his mole, she was passing on information about the alien wreck on Ghayth.

Bram sat in the visitors' gallery of the courtroom, watching the ebb and flow of the people beyond the bar.

Called to the bar. He knew that meant something to some folks; however, to him, it meant you had to be "someone" to go beyond the waist-high barrier separating the visitors' gallery from the working part of the courtroom on the other side.

There, on the far right, was the jurors' box— empty today. The prosecutors sat next at a short row of tables, separated by a gap of less than ten feet from the defense tables that also held the accused. The judges were going to be seated up on top of that dais at the center of the room with their backs against the Anulet red-and-white wood wall, the parquet tiles so small that the wall looked almost crimson.

All of the seats, including those in the gallery, were covered in a pure white fabric and made out of a solid-looking wood. *Looks like oak,* he thought.

Wait, maybe black walnut. I really have no idea. But a courtroom should look like a place where justice is served, and this is such a place.

As usual, the person accused of a criminal act would be presented, and the prosecutor would be expected to prove the guilt of the accused. However, today would be different. Yes, someone was the accused, but as he pictured Gia Scott, he realized that the accused in this case was guilty. Everyone knew that. Everyone had seen her shoot three people. She had killed the Master Adept and Duke David d'Avigdor and wounded Tanner Scott.

Bram had been a member of the wedding party at Tanner's wedding, and he had been as close as one could possibly be to the shooting. Even discounting his eyes and memory, there were vids from many of the news and vid stations that proved her guilt.

He sighed. In spite of all the evidence, there were "mitigating circumstances" that meant there might be a way for her crime to be modified and the penalty for same to be adjusted or reduced.

At least he hoped so.

When a man Bram thought was the bailiff entered the courtroom, all talking in the visitors' gallery ceased. A quick look inside the man's head proved him right, and the bailiff asked all to stand as the judge was coming in.

Shortly thereafter, a judge appeared in a crimson

robe with a dark fur collar and took his seat. He was a man of indeterminate age, but past fifty for sure, with a balding head, and he wore old-fashioned glasses perched well down his nose. He looked over the top of the rim of his glasses and nodded at the court bailiff.

Moments later, from behind the dais on the other side, in paraded the defense first—a young man who must be Gia's lawyer followed by a Provost guard holding Gia's arm. As they settled in at the defense table, the prosecutor came in, looking like he was in a hurry, and quickly dropped a big pile of folders and two tablets onto his table. He looked over at a woman who sat below the judge's dais, smiled, and made motions to her that Bram couldn't see clearly.

A quick look inside the prosecutor's brain showed him little, as the man was nudging around a song in his head, purposely keeping Bram and any other Issians out of the loop.

Whatever he had asked the clerk was relayed to the judge, who sat up straighter in his seat, Bram thought, and he looked around the visitors' gallery. There were five news anchors up front already, and he saw a vid camera, which would be recording a feed for everyone's usage later. Sitting beside him was a courtroom artist already drawing a picture of the setup here in the courtroom. Bram thought he'd made Gia's hair a bit too dark, but that was okay with the big wavy style the artist had done.

The judge spoke up, his voice as empty of emotion as one could hope. "Let's get started, shall we," he said, as he looked down through his glasses at whatever lay in front of him.

The prosecutor rose, walked up to the lectern that stood between the defense's table and his table, and smiled up at the judge. "Your Honor, we have scheduled today for a simple motions hearing—for various motions on the upcoming trial of the defendant, one Gia Scott, on the charges of double murder in the first degree.

"We would ask that these motions are all decided upon before a suitable court date to start the trial could be arranged.

"We also ask that the defendant be held in remand until that date can be—"

"Your Honor, please, I object. Instead of dealing with the introduction at hand, the prosecution is asking for a decision up front before we've even begun to argue for habeas corpus," the defense lawyer almost shouted as he rose and leaned forward, his hands holding himself up on his table.

His name, Bram knew, was Jordan Alpert. He was a Barony citizen who had applied for and received quick approvals to practice law here on Neen, the capital planet of the Duchy d'Avigdor.

25

He knew too that this little tip toward speed had been given by Helena, Tanner's wife, who now as the Duchess d'Avigdor, a Royal, had simply asked that this be done by the Duchy Law Society. Unusual, yes. Unprecedented, no. It had been done often on many RIM Confederacy worlds, as lawyers sometimes followed their clients from realm to realm. Still, the young man was new to the Duchy d'Avigdor, and it remained to be seen if he could work around his unknowns and change the current charges and sentence for Gia.

Hope he can, Bram thought, *and I might be the only guy here in this court who would want that.*

The judge nodded at the defense. "Sustained, and Mr. Alpert, no need to jump with force, young man," he said dryly.

The defense lawyer sat.

The prosecutor nodded. "Sorry, Your Honor, back to the motions. The prosecution has only three to offer up today. The first of which is that," he said as he nodded to a second lawyer on the prosecution's team who stood and trotted over to the defense table and then to the court clerk to deliver printed documents.

The prosecutor continued. "We would like a ruling, please, on the level of interference that this case will enjoy—we ask that as the defendant is a blood relative of the new duke that no Royals be

26

allowed to attend or testify at the trial. We do not need them to do that—there are valid verified videos that show all the evidence we will need," he said.

Alpert was up on his feet at once. "Your Honor, we object once again. While the use of these videos will be argued later, the fact that the prosecution wishes to limit the role that either the duke or his wife might play in this trial is beyond what he can ask for. We, the defense, might want to call one or both of them.

"There were dozens of other Royals attending the wedding, and many of them were up front in the front row. Surely, the prosecution would have no issue with any of them being called by us as well.

"But the duke and his wife, being closest to the scene, would be perhaps of great value to us in the defense of this defendant. Perhaps they saw something that we all missed—that the unverified videos missed too. Surely, Your Honor, you can not countenance that action ..." he said, once again leaning forward on his table.

Alpert shook his head. "More than that, Your Honor, we also object to his use of the term 'interference' in relation to this case and its intent to pre-poison Your Honor's mind to the value of a Royal and their testimony. Surely, Your Honor, justice is blind ..." he said, and that got a slight grin on the judge's face that was so fleeting, Bram didn't know if he'd seen it—or just felt it with his mind.

"Sustained. Mister Prosecutor, we will not limit any Royal in any way in this case. You or the defense may call them as witnesses should you desire to do that. Clerk, so ordered, please record that motion. Next, if you please ..." he said dryly.

The prosecutor nodded to his second, and again documents were trotted around to the defense's table and the clerk's table.

The prosecutor began speaking while Alpert looked over the documents. "We also make the motion that due to the fact that the defendant is related to the duke—who at the time was Lord Scott of the Barony—that any and all medical records from the Barony Hospital Ship be marked as inadmissible in our courts. The bias that such records might show would be highly biased and prejudicial in that they may try to show the defendant as non compos mentis to validate those records as exculpatory evidence."

The judge held up his hand and stopped the defense attorney who was already leaping to his feet. "Let me have this one, young man," he said as he smiled down at the prosecutor.

"Not a chance, Mister Prosecutor, as medical records are always admissible. They come from professionals who went to school for longer than you or I did—so that motion, too, Clerk, is to be recorded as denied. Next, please ..." he said as he motioned for Alpert to resume his seat.

"Lastly, then, Your Honor, we ask that the courtroom be closed to any and all Issians, as their attendance would be a detriment to the prosecution, in that it would allow the Issians to be aware of, and therefore able to take advantage of, prosecution strategy before it even occurs, Your Honor," he said as he half-turned toward Bram.

Bram was dressed in his Duchy d'Avigdor whites, and the navy uniform included, of course, his Adept officer badging of the ringed planet. Bram shifted slightly in his seat. *Not a chance,* he thought, and he smiled up at the judge, who was now looking at him.

Neither the defense lawyer nor the judge said anything for a moment, so Bram rose. As he did, the bailiff trundled over to stand in front of him, blocking his way to move past the bar.

Bram shook his head, moved to one side, got the attention of the judge, and said, "May I speak to that, Your Honor?"

The judge frowned and peered over the rim of his glasses at the Issian in front of him. "Are you related to the defendant?" he asked.

"No, Your Honor, in fact, I've never even met the defendant," he said in all honesty.

He could feel her eyes staring at him, and he glanced away from the judge to look at her for a second and then looked back at the judge.

"Have you made a personal determination of the guilt or innocence of the defendant?" the judge asked.

"Not at all, Your Honor," he replied.

The judge looked down at the defense and the prosecution and then posed his last question. "And were you friendly with the Master Adept who the defendant has been charged with murdering?"

"Yes, Your Honor. Like all Issians, I respected and in fact loved the Master. And I would ask that you allow us—those of us who wish to come to the trial—to be able to come and see justice done. Barring Issians is so unfair, so un-duchy-like that I would think that might change the relations between Eons and Neen, Your Honor. We seek what justice we can ..." he said.

Bram felt he'd taken the right road in this argument. He knew the judge was on the fence, but surely cutting off the Issians from even attending the court as visitors would be a bad thing.

"Further, your Honor," Alpert said as he rose, "is the standing precedent that is followed by all courts in the RIM Confederacy that no Issian—in fact no one of any faith, color, race, gender, or religion—be barred from any court proceedings. Surely, Your

Honor, this last prosecution motion seeks to break with court tradition. And then there's the whole issue of appeals and what that motion, if successful, would do for the judge who found it fitting to enact same," he said.

The judge looked at him. His face was stern and showed that he didn't fear appeals. Yet he did, Bram could see, and that argument from Gia's lawyer seemed to win the judge over.

Bram sat and as he did, he could still see Gia looking at him, measuring him somehow, her brain was saying. He smiled at her—a small smile—and got the same back as she turned to face the judge who was about to rule.

"Motion denied, Mister Prosecutor. Clerk, record same, please, and issue the docs soonest to both sides. Is that all for the prosecution?" he asked.

Bram thought the prosecutor looked a bit flustered as he sat, and then as the man agreed with the judge, the defense lawyer stood and took his place at the lectern.

"Your Honor, we have only one motion at this time," the defense lawyer said as the courtroom grew quiet.

"We make the motion of habeas corpus at this time, Your Honor. We know that the defendant is currently being held in the Neen County Jail in solitary and as such enjoys little time for counsel and working with us on her defense. What we would like to ask is that the courts allow the defendant—innocent until proven guilty, mind you —to take up residence within the ducal palace. Fully guarded by the Duchy d'Avigdor Navy Provost core—a collateral force within the duchy court system. She would be chipped, and she would be able to help greatly with her own case. We ask, Your Honor, as we all know that this woman here today is innocent."

The prosecutor was up on his feet in less than a second and waved an arm up and down as if he was a traffic officer stopping vehicles during rush hour.

The judge interrupted him before a full word left his mouth. "Wait, before your objection, Mister Prosecutor—are you aware that the defendant is being held in full solitary confinement in the Neen County Jail?"

"I am conversant with those facts, Your Honor," he said as he stood at the prosecution table.

"Are you also aware that there is a shortage— quite a sizable shortage, I understand—with the COs there—the correctional officers," the judge said, now looking down at the tablet in front of him, "and that gives her only two hours a day for visitors —lawyer included?"

The prosecutor was waving furiously at his

assistant attorney who was rummaging through folder after folder looking for paperwork to perhaps refute that statement.

"And are you aware that the defendant is—like all defendants are—presumed to be innocent until proven guilty?" the judge asked.

Bram smiled.

The defense lawyer in front of him and to his left smiled too—well, he couldn't see the lawyer's face, but he knew a smile when he saw it in a brain within reach.

"Clerk, I'm going to grant this defense motion. The defendant is hereby remanded, in house arrest, let's call it, to the duchy palace; rooms et cetera to be decided upon by the Duchy Navy Provost guard. They are charged with the duty of keeping her at that location, subject to changes that the courts might deem necessary until trial.

"They are to chip the defendant and remove all ID papers, passports, any and all kinds of travel documents. They are also to issue daily reports to the clerk of this court on the verified whereabouts of the defendant at all times. No exceptions. No mistakes.

"I want the duke notified of this—and the admiral of the Duchy Navy as well as the commandant of the Duchy Navy Provost Guard.

"No mistakes, Miss—do you read me?" the judge

said, addressing Gia for the first time.

Bram looked toward Gia who nodded and said, "Yes, Your Honor."

"Good, Clerk, issue docs to all—don't forget the duke et al. either," he said as he rose.

The bailiff hustled back up to the front and yelled, "All rise for the superior court judge," as the judge left the courtroom

Bram stayed standing, and as he turned to the aisle down the row of seats, he looked over at Gia. She stared at him, and he received one thought, beamed over to him like she was trying to send him a message. *"Who are you..."* was the only thought he received.

Hunting Guide Master Koenig bowed fully from the waist, stepped forward, and grinned at Tanner as he clasped the duke's forearm in his hand. He gripped it as if it was a lifesaver ring to a drowning man. "Duke—so, so good to see you again," he said as he released that half-crushed forearm and then bowed once more.

Tanner grinned and said, "No, no, Guide Master, no bowing to this duke ..." He reached out to try to straighten up the man, and that was a hardship he'd not encountered before.

The man was at least fifteen years older than

Tanner, but what he grabbed was all muscle, tendon, and bone. *Not an ounce of fat,* Tanner thought, *Koenig is more in shape than men half his age.* Tanner led the guide master over to the seating area, and they settled on the facing divans in the palace salon.

Since he'd been the duke—only about a month—Tanner felt the seating in the salon was too formalized, too comfortable, and much too soft. Not surprisingly, he heard about it right away.

"This is a bit of a soft room, eh, Duke?" Koenig said as he pushed down on the seat cushion beside where he sat. The springs below made no sound, but the cushion went down at least a foot.

"Agreed, Guide Master," Tanner said, but he waved off any follow-up comment and got right to the point. "I have decided that—well, that my groomsmen from my wedding of more than a year ago need something more. What happened," he said as they both nodded to each other, "was a tragedy, and yet I think that my friends will need some kind of closure, I think they call it. Something else to remember rather than the deaths of the Master Adept and Duke David."

The guide master nodded but did not interrupt. Wearing the traditional browns and greens, the forest shades of Anulet, he was dressed as he always was. Tanner noted that his holster on his

35

side was empty, but that didn't mean Koenig was at anyone's mercy—the reputation that this Anulet citizen carried was that he was as deadly unarmed as armed.

"So, what I'm planning is a hunt for us all—on Anulet, of course, and for Oved. Those bigger than elk huge beasts should be in their rut in the next few weeks, and that kind of mating fire makes for a great hunt, right?"

The guide master nodded and then answered his duke. "Yes, this is prime Oved hunting season for about the next month. Glad to see you know that— but a caution, Duke? Summer season has been tough on Anulet. We had some pretty severe drought conditions, which made the Oved forage areas smaller.

"Compacted them really, especially near the canyons that you might remember. So that made them easy pickings for the Jaels who decided that they too like Oved meat. Numbers are down somewhat, and few young will make it to their first birthdays but that shouldn't affect our hunt at all. Mounted, Sir?" he asked.

Tanner had used Gallipedia to look up more on Anulet than he thought he'd ever want to know— but mounted on what was not a part of what he'd read.

"Your advice there, guide master?" he asked.

36

Royals who don't know pretend to know, he reasoned as he cocked his head as if ready to accept counsel and consider same.

"Duke, yes, mounted is perhaps best in the best of times—but as the hard summer has concentrated the Oveds into fewer square miles, we can easily hunt on foot. Dogs though could be used to help move the Oved toward us in some cases, but yes, I would say we do not need horses this time," he said.

Tanner now remembered they called the mounts horses, but the creatures were solid purple with six legs; they were definitely not the horses he thought he knew.

"Agreed, Guide Master. Let's choose some dates, shall we?" he asked as he reached for his tablet on the coffee table in front of him. He noted the guide master didn't have a tablet and asked, "Do you want to perhaps delay the choice of dates, Guide Master, until you have your schedule handy?"

Koenig tapped the side of his head and grinned. "Duke, when the head of state decides on a date— all others get moved or canceled. That I know, so what dates have you considered, Sir?"

Tanner recognized that was another Royal trait he'd need to brush up on. "In two weeks, let's say— arrival and orientation day one, hunt days two and three, and depart after a final banquet on day three.

Will that work for you?" he asked.

"We will make it work for you, the Duke d'Avigdor. Might I ask—will there be needs to arm all the guests, or shall that be done here from the ducal armory?"

"Here is good," Tanner said, and that alone would be a fun afternoon, he knew.

"Then we will look for you then, Duke—fourteen days from today. I will ensure the main lodge has rooms ready and our best fare for your guests, Sir," he said as he rose and bowed once again from the waist.

Watching the guide master stride out of the salon, Tanner was struck once again with the power in the man's step and the hope that he might be just as fit when he was at that age.

He looked down at the tablet, made some additions to the notes, and then said, "Ayla, could you come in, please?"

It hadn't taken but one EYES ONLY to ask his aide Ayla to join him. He had asked her to leave the Barony Navy and accept the same rank in the Duchy Navy. Helena had prompted him to at least ask.

Tanner felt a slight twinge of guilt that he was always "poaching" staff from wherever he had just left. But his wife had pointed out that those who knew him wanted to be on the "Tanner bandwagon," and if that meant they left their old position to take a new one with him, so be it.

Ayla came into the salon and nodded before he could even say a word to her. "Your Grace, yes, I was monitoring from the side anteroom and will make the needed calls and arrange for the *Sword* to make the milk-run to go and get all the groomsmen who can attend the hunt two weeks less a day from today.

"I will also schedule the armorer to be in attendance down in the armory to help your guests choose weapons as well, Your Grace. And I will make sure to double-check with the Grand Hunting Lodge on Anulet about numbers as well. Do you as yet have any choices for the final night's banquet menu?" she asked.

Tanner grunted. *She should be the duke,* he thought as he shook his head negatively. "Not in the least—other than perhaps it should be something traditionally Anulet in style and substance, Ayla?"

She nodded "Excellent choice, Your Grace. I will get back to you later today with a list of items, and I'll include some Gallipedia links too for background should there be something that might not be apparent with the recipes and ingredients, Your Grace."

He nodded and she left him alone. As he sat there, he realized that not only was he poaching people—people whom he liked and had formed relationships with—but the *Sword*, too, was his once again. His minister in charge of—*Something. What was it*, he thought. *Ah, never mind.* The man had been able to get a great deal from the Barony Navy on the big shuttle, and so the *Sword* had become the newest addition to the Duchy Navy.

He rose and went over to the small butler's pantry on the side of the room opposite the enormous formal windows. Reaching into the cold cabinet, he pulled out a bottle of water and took a big sip. He walked toward the windows and looked outside even though Helena was up on the top floor of the palace, waiting for him. There were probably many ways to reach that floor, but he knew of only the one. Out the door, turn left, go all the way down the hallway, and then take the stairs, two at a time, up to the third floor. On the third floor, go past the stationed Provost guard who saluted each and every time and down the long corridor to the final stairs up to the residential suites above.

"Gotta be more ways than that," he said to himself as he sipped the water and looked out across the palace grounds toward Neen City, the capital of the Duchy d'Avigdor. While hard to see, if he squinted just a bit, he could barely make out the streams of flying cars well above the streets below. Once in awhile, a car would dive off on an angle as it began to descend and the big front headlights shone his way for an instant, and he smiled once more.

It was the end almost of the evening rush hour as citizens left their workplaces to return home.

"Me too," he said to himself, promising to ask the palace AI to give him a working model of the palace corridors and hallways and put it on his PDA. *Makes me more of a duke*, he thought, and he grinned as he turned away from the rush hour and toward his own residence.

Captain Magnusson was impressed—no two ways about it. He'd been met at a private doorway to the Barony Palace by an EliteGuard—a major, in fact—and escorted through seven different rooms, down four more hallways, and up three escalators and down yet another to end up here—in a meeting with the Baroness.

It was supposed to be a meeting, but so far, he sat alone on the divan the Elite Guard had directed him to. The major now stood over on the far side of the spacious receiving room, at attention, and Captain Magnusson continued to wait.

Wall hangings were plentiful. *Old tapestry type of welted weaving,* he thought, and they showed everything from the moons over Eons to the hunt of

41

a Jael on Anulet. *Impressive,* he thought as his eyes drifted to the right, and in doing so, he must have missed the entry of the Baroness because she was now sitting down opposite him on her own chocolate divan.

He jumped up, went to attention, and said, "My Lady, Captain Mel Magnusson, reporting as ordered."

She nodded and waved for him to sit on the couch again. "Yes, yes, Captain. Please, sit yourself —refreshments, please, AI," she said.

From somewhere behind him, he could hear a door open, and in came a steward with a cart. On it were many kinds of pastries, muffins, and tarts; there were also pitchers of juices and a thermos of coffee. But like all non-Royals, he waited until his Baroness had spoken first.

"I'll have a nice Bundi juice, please—with one of those butter tarts with the raisins," she said as she looked at him.

He said, "Coffee, black, please," and the cup appeared on the table in front of him, a silver spoon still nestled in the saucer. He didn't pick it up until she reached for her tall, misted glass of bright blue juice and smiled at him.

She wore an outfit in unique colors, but like everyone else, he had no real idea what colors the Baroness wore. Chartreuse came to mind, but that was too yellow to describe her top and leggings. The boots might have been chartreuse, but the clothing had a touch of violet mixed in.

Her long locks had been pulled back tautly, and two long tresses had a matching ribbon of the same color as her boots wrapped around them. He knew little about makeup, but she looked like she could go right to a state dinner. She was about as impressive a beauty as he'd ever seen.

He knew he had to watch himself around women, and adding in the beauty of this one, and he would need to be on guard at all times. He considered trying to make small talk, but the Baroness leaned forward, put down the now half-empty glass of juice, and picked up the butter tart on a small side plate in front of her. She nibbled a bit on one edge and then pointed at him with the same hand holding the tart, one forefinger outstretched.

"You, Captain Magnusson, are the Barony Navy captain who took it upon himself to take our yet-to-be-launched Barony Drive out for a shakedown test cruise—more than a thousand lights, I understand —with no permission from anyone," she said calmly,.

He was surprised but she did have the goods on him. He had done just that—taken the *BN Exeter* to Branton, the home world of Duke d'Avigdor—

then an admiral in the Barony Navy—on a lark. The Barony Drive had worked perfectly, and after positioning the satellite around that world's sun, the trip home too was a success.

"Had it not worked, you'd have faced a trip for, what, three-and-some years to come home. But it did work," she said.

She took another bite of the tart, which was now almost gone. Captain Magnusson opened his mouth to speak to that, but she held up her hand holding the tart once again.

"Congratulations, Captain. I like navy officers who show gumption, and you certainly did that," she said as she popped the last of that tart into her mouth and reached for the juice to wash it all down. She dusted her lips with the small square napkin that had accompanied the tart, and she brushed any crumbs off her hands.

Time, he thought, *to answer her.*

But again she went on, and he bit his tongue to stop.

"I like that action—which means that I like you, Captain. And, as you are what I'd call a navy man with ambition—I have a special mission for you. A confidential mission—one that might be fraught with danger but might not too. I have no idea, but it involves Pentyaan space. Is that something you might consider, Captain?"

44

He nodded and finally got to speak. "Yes, Ma'am! The trip to Branton was a test, really, of the capacity of the Barony Drive—and it worked out fine. You might remember that months later, it was the *Exeter* and my crew that were sent to test the range of the drive, and we established that the Barony Drive worked perfectly as it was supposed to for up to at least ten thousand lights, Ma'am. So, with Pentyaan space being only about fifty lights from Neres, I have no problem at all, Ma'am," he said.

She nodded but held up a hand, palm facing him. "Yes, but this is not a simple test. In fact, you and your crew will know about this mission, as will I — but no one else.

"Here's the background, Captain. Years ago, when Captain Rossum and her ship appeared with the Roma gypsies and asked for refugee status— you will remember, that happened just before the battle with the reaper aliens over on Memories?"

He nodded. He knew and he was still a bit nonplussed as the *Exeter* had not been a part of that task force.

"When we took over the gypsy ship, we transferred all their cargo and personal effects to the naval base here on Neres. A part of what we stored were ore and rock samples they had found along their trading routes. From moons and asteroids and planets—each carefully cataloged and coordinates recorded as to where they had been found.

"One of those samples, a dull red ore, was found on an asteroid around a barren world in Pentyaan space. Sometime perhaps a billion years ago, a meteorite had smashed into the asteroid and half-buried itself in the crust of same. We tested that sample—as a matter of course, we tested all the samples they had found—and we are very interested in that red ore.

"We want you—well, the *Exeter*—to go and find that asteroid and that meteorite strike and mine that ore for us. We need as much as you can find and bring back, Captain—and all at TOP SECRET level too. Not a word to anyone—but me, Captain. Interested?" she asked as she downed the glass of juice and waved at the steward across the room for more.

As the steward hustled forward, Magnusson was silent until the newly filled glass was full and the steward had returned to his post far enough away to not overhear.

"Ma'am, I'd be honored to carry this out for you. Say the word and as soon as I have coordinates, we're off," he said.

She nodded as she sipped the blue juice, and he waited for almost a minute.

"Fine, Captain. I will send you the needed

information, via the *Exeter*, and it will be on your console before you even get back to the base," she said, still sipping blue juice from her glass. "But there is a deadline—we need the ore as soon as possible—no later than, say, a month from today ..."

He nodded and took a sip of the coffee. It was strong, black, and had a taste he'd never tried before —almost like chocolate and luwak flavored at the same time. Of course, it would be the best, and he took another sip of the still very hot coffee.

"You like the coffee," she asked, her head tilting to one side with a smile.

He grinned at her and said, "Oh, yes, Ma'am, this is wonderful." There was nothing else to say as it truly was just that.

She nodded and while he didn't catch a gesture, the EliteGuard major was now standing off to his left.

He cleared his throat.

"Captain, if you'd accompany me, please, once again," the guard said and he knew the meeting was over.

As he walked with the guard, retracing his steps, he realized this mission was outside of the normal navy flow of rank and orders. He'd have to find a way to let his admiral know that he was off into Pentyaan space—somehow—without spilling the beans ...

The RIM CONFEDERACY: Captured Aliens

CHAPTER TWO

Major Stal sat bewildered at first. He'd been told about a new find on Ghayth, something that was both unexpected and hidden but right in front of anyone who approached the spot from the south. Due south.

As the shuttle once again did a flyover of the tip of the landmass pointing directly south to the Ghayth south pole, he could see nothing different from what he expected to see. This was the tip of the southernmost continent on the planet and here it narrowed as it fell into the sea. Still, at least a few thousand feet wide before ending on the cliffs that the sea now crashed upon, it was a brutal land for sure. Two peaks jutted up a few hundred feet from the tailing into the sea range of cliffs.

More high ragged peaks with slides of rubble and

49

scree and whole layers of the rock substructure were sliding off the final cliffs. It'd take centuries for the rubble to clear so that the layers underneath would then be treated to the rains and storms to crack and then become rubble themselves. The rocks he saw were all of the hard granite type, plutonic, he thought they were called, where they cooled slowly over millennia even. But what was even stranger was that he could actually see the cliffs, the rocks, and the sea itself here.

"Pilot, put the audit tape on from one year ago— these coordinates, please?" he said to the pilot who sat on his right.

The lieutenant nodded, and moments later, the big view-screen up front split in half. The left side showed the view from the shuttle, and the right side held the same view but from one year ago when the drones had flown this same area.

Today, he could see everything in the gray cloudy day.

But from a year ago, there was nothing to see at all. Gray skies too, but the skies were filled with driving rain in sheets. There was a hint from below of the edge of the cliff maybe, but he couldn't be sure. There were no twin peaks either, which today stuck up a few hundred feet above the range of cliffs—but back a year ago were just a gray mass.

"Looks like the changes that the science guys are

working on work," the pilot said, and Alver grunted a yes.

The pilot turned hard to starboard and zoomed down to about twice the height of the cliffs. He continued to turn in a big circle to come back at the cliffs from due south. "Major, this is the view you gotta see," he said as he leveled out about two miles away.

As the shuttle now flew directly at the end of the landmass, those twin peaks ahead changed. They seemed to move away from each other and dip slightly backward from this angle and away from the cliffs and the sea.

"What the hell," Alver said as he leaned forward to get a better look.

"Navy science guys think that those two peaks ain't real. On gimbals maybe, that have some kind of a motion detector built in and turned on. Approach from anywhere other than due south, and they ignore you," the pilot said.

Alver nodded and as they moved at moderate speed toward the now separating peaks, what lay below was now not hidden anymore.

The space below was lit with some kind of light source he couldn't see. The space appeared to be a landing field, big enough to hold four shuttles of this size. The landing field was covered with some markings in spots too, and Alver recognized the writing—it was from the ancient aliens who'd come to Ghayth thousands of years ago.

He held up a hand for the pilot to stop over the field. He fluttered his hand back and forth, signifying for the shuttle to hover, and the pilot complied.

From up here, Alver could see there appeared to be a whole interior below-grade plateau, buried down at least a few hundred feet below the level of the cliffs to the south. From up here, he could still see fortifications, equipment, dollies, stacks of something on skids, and enormous interior panels of glass that looked like the walls of interior rooms. He really had no idea.

"And how, as a matter of fact, was this discovered?" he asked, but he thought he knew.

"Normal annual audit drones. One was acting wonky, the autopilot said, and he took it out for a spin around and came back from the south. Due south, the GPS said, and that got those peaks a-moving and voila," the pilot said.

Alver nodded. *Figures*, he thought. *We stumble into this kind of thing too, too often here on Ghayth; sure would be nice to know more.*

Then he sighed. Not knowing what a planet had in store for its first immigrants was something all space-faring races ran into ... and Ghayth was no different.

"Okay, home, Lieutenant, and don't spare the horses," he said.

As the pilot zoomed up to go sub-orbital, Alver saw the twin peaks behind them slowly rise up to once again hide the outpost or whatever lay below. As the shuttle hit Mach 2 and then Mach 3, aiming up still, Alver had to decide whom to share this with.

Found by Barony Navy drones, handled by both the science team here as well as now the marines, of which he was the CC on the planet, meant it was not going to be a secret much longer.

Wish I had Tanner here to tell him—even if that is ethically a bad choice, Alver thought. He was a Barony marine—and had sworn an oath to be just that.

If ever the chance might come up to even hint at this to the new duke, I'd take it—maybe ... or maybe not ...

As she ambled along the walkway, number nineteen, she thought she'd heard Professor Reynolds, head of her xeno team on the alien wreck on Ghayth, call it, she looked around. And up. And far to her left, and far to her right. And then she stopped.

"Professor—tell me again? If a ship is used to transport people or things from planet to planet—

why then does this ship have such huge interior wide-open space? Nothing is 'in' here but air. Sure, I see the openings all over as I look up and around —but of what value might this unused space be to these aliens?" the Baroness asked, her voice a bit frustrated.

Reynolds nodded as he stopped and swung a hand in a circle. "Ma'am, the space that we see as unused—may be a very necessary part of the ship to aliens who fly. Perhaps it might be a space where they can take wing and, say, 'stretch' their wings. Perhaps it was used to hold thousands of these aliens all on those 'alien ladders' we've found—a way to house aliens with wings. Perhaps we just will never understand it. But one thing we do know is that all of those openings up and around this space have perches at the doorstep—so to speak. So the aliens flew to those rooms—whatever kind of room it was," he said.

He too was unknowing when it came to the real reason for the vast open space in the middle axis of the ship, but like all academics, he put that aside for now. The knowing might come long after the finding, was how a professor of one of his undergrad classes had put it to him more than forty years ago. *How true,* he thought, but he did wonder why that might be important to the Baroness, but of course, one never asked a Royal to explain themselves or their questions.

She nodded. She was not satisfied with his answer, he knew, but he really didn't have one. "Let's move on," she said.

He led the way ahead. When they reached a juncture of a side-branching walkway, she stopped. "And where does that lead," she said, pointing at the walkway that appeared to lead hundreds of yards away from this spot.

"We, as yet, don't know, Ma'am. When a xeno team explores, it's done by us all—full video captures and, yes, even a squad of marines as well. That one is labeled," he said as he peered down at the floor where the two walkways intersected, "as walkway number 133—with an extra icon behind that number. We've no idea what that icon signifies either yet, Ma'am—though that one is scheduled to be investigated next month, I believe."

She looked at him, as she cocked each hand on a hip, one shapely leg in thigh-high boots canted off to one side. "Wait, Professor. Do you mean that there are many parts of the ship that you've not even been to as yet?"

"Yes, Ma'am. We've covered only about twenty-eight percent of the ship from what we can tell. Those areas covered, however, we know. We have indexed and cataloged. We understand and have tested and worked on all hypotheses that we can discern as to what and why they are here on the ship. We go slowly, Ma'am, not so much for our own safety—but to prevent doing anything catastrophic by accident. Via ignorance or stupidity, Ma'am. It's the xeno way of discovering a whole new race of aliens—and judging by what we've found, these were very superior aliens, technology-wise."

She just looked at him and frowned. "Surely, you want to just run down all of these walkways, as you call them, and look and see and find stuff, right?"

He grinned at her, as he nodded too. "Aye, Ma'am—we all do. It takes quite a bit of stick-tuitiveness to NOT do just that. But we know that our way works.

"Do you remember what happened up on the moons of Thrones just a dozen or more years ago, Ma'am?"

She shook her head as she motioned for him to proceed down the walkway ahead.

"Ah, well, Ma'am, I was on that xeno team called to investigate the remains of a satellite that had somehow been wrecked on the Thrones2 planetary system—on their moon. We went everywhere and branched off and took working escalators up and down ... almost running to see and begin to understand what we had found. All went well at first, until one of us on the bridge was punching on icons and items. Nothing seemed to make any changes to the satellite that we could see, which was decided later at the post-mortem of the xeno team reports.

"No, we looked and spread out, and we dug and we forged ahead, and we entered the big remains — only to have a self-security system decide — for whatever reason it did — that we were invaders, and it automatically fired upon us with no warning. We never even found the thresholds that we'd breached — it just sent automatic plasma fire down the corridor towards us — and at the same time, we could hear the slow drone of what sounded like 'tick-tocks' as there was an automatic counter that was enabled by our breach. At least that's what was determined later after the plasma blasts."

She gasped. "What happened?"

"We lost four of the team that day — plasma took them full on as they were in the lead team positions as we were moving down the main corridor of the satellite. We realized the counter mechanism might signify something else was also triggered, so we all bailed out. We got up and into space about twenty miles away, when there was a huge flash of light, and the shockwave tumbled our shuttle somewhat too. The crater was almost a full mile across — and everything else within that blast radius was now just moon dust."

She took that in. He had been honest with his reference to this event, and yes, she'd read the complete reports on same in her research on xeno teams. It had been his own culpability in the handling of the information after the fact, which had made her think he'd be the one to head this team. She'd not been wrong, it appeared, as she said nothing but continued to follow Reynolds as the walkway ahead disappeared into a new large opening.

"This is the area we call the rear cargo hold—one of at least the thirty-one that we've identified. Oh, that number—thirty-one—seems to be important to these aliens too. Many, many items that we see replicated, stacked, or identified—all are done in only thirty-one items.

"We don't know if that's a base of their math— we humans use a base-ten math or something else. But thirty-one is important, it seems," he said as he stepped across the threshold and into a large cargo bay room.

On the far wall was what appeared to be a closed and sealed door allowing someone or something to open same, take or place cargo within the room, and then close up and seal it off from space. Inside the massive hundred-foot-ceiling-height room were boxes, cylinders, pipe lengths, and round barrels of items that all looked like they were brand new and still sealed. She pointed at same.

"Professor, I have read your team reports and noted that you believe that the age of this wreck — and its contents, I would add — are around twenty thousand years old. If so, then why are these cargo containers still so pristine looking? Not a single broken or rusted or cracked-open barrel do I see."

Reynolds nodded and spread his hands out, palms up as if shrugging with his hands. "Ma'am, we just don't know. But what we do know is that this wreck still is powered. There are occasional periods in the day when automatic things happen.

"Lights go on or off; up in what we think are personnel quarters, there are automatic air changes within the rooms, and the teeniest of robo-cleaners appear to vacuum up not the floors but the perches and what we think are food dishes.

"Down in other areas, there are larger robots who ignore us completely and appear to be doing some kind of inventory as they motor along each row of boxes, flashing out what looks like a barcode reader to inventory the goods it finds.

"But no matter what is on automatic, we've yet to see any evidence of any kind of rot or succumbing to time by anything we've found — as yet, Ma'am. I doubt that we will, but other xeno team members think differently, Ma'am," he said, and his tone conveyed he didn't believe those team members.

Ahead of her, he walked over to a stack of boxes, made out of some type of metal, that stood about three feet high, and he pushed the stack enough that the top box fell off. He backed up and held out a hand for her to be still.

After almost a full minute, she could heard a something motorized coming toward them from around the corner. It was a robot. It looked like one at least, and it ignored her and the four EliteGuards who'd accompanied them as it made its way to the fallen box.

Her EliteGuard team leader had already drawn his sidearm, but she waved him to stop to watch.

The robot reached the box and seemed to be studying the situation; then it reached out a clawed appendage, picked up the box, placed it on top of the pile, and balanced it there. Two other claw hands appeared from its interior somehow, and they gently straightened the pile of boxes back into perfect alignment. As the arms withdrew back into its interior, a beam of light lanced out to read the codes on that box now replaced and then down the rest of the boxes in that row. All must have been well, as the beam of light suddenly disappeared, and the robot did a full swivel on its caterpillar treads and went back the way it had come.

"All of the cargo bays—well, the five we've investigated and indexed and cataloged, that is, work like this too. Interesting, yes?" he asked, and he got a nod back.

Very interesting, she thought and looked around the cargo hold. Opened up any of these as yet?" she inquired, but she felt she knew what the answer was going to be.

"Not yet, Ma'am. When we took down some to figure out how to open them—those cargo-bots appeared and re-stacked them on their own. We figure that we'll bring in some anti-grav plates, hoist some cargo containers on same, and then move them out of the holds to see what's in them. That's scheduled, I know, for next month at the earliest, I believe. And yes, Ma'am, another example of 'stumbling' onto something that we did not foresee ahead of time. Lucky that there was no crater this time," he said, almost apologetically.

She said, "Lets' go back to the tents, shall we?" and they all turned and left the cargo bay. As they did, the lights dimmed on the ship's AI as it now knew there were no visitors within the cargo bay.

On the walk back, the Baroness didn't talk at all; instead she was thinking about just how long it was going to take to find out if the wreck held any usable secrets. She'd been more than happy with the contents of the arctic warehouse—and had been able to use some of same almost immediately. The new Barony Drive used the copper and blue anti-grav plates to make travel here almost instantaneous, and there had been thousands of matched sets.

Major Stal was in the process of looking into another find, and she was awaiting word back from him today. But all in all, Ghayth had become a mine of its own; she needed to find more gold in same was her thought for the day. Maybe she could make a real addition to the Barony ... from ancient aliens.

Bram knew this was a chance he'd not get again. He waited beside the long curtain on the kiosk that sold fresh fruits at Dessau city center. Capital of Eons, the city of Dessau had an open-air farmer's market that was open all days, and today, he partially hid behind the edge of the kiosk, between the curtain and the big stack of melons.

The market today was full of citizens. Some bought food to take home or snack items to eat now. Others purchased clothing and gift items from the large craft area on one side.

For more than five hundred years, the market had been set up where the main street in the city met the central city square. Vehicles were still permitted to run on the other side of the street, and Bram watched carefully. He was soon rewarded with the sight of the Issian car that carried the Master Adept as it pulled up. Moments later, she was on the curb, out of the large car, and looking around.

Rather quickly, she turned and stared directly at him as she felt him with her mind. In his head, using mind speak, she said, *"Come over, yes, Bram ..."* She motioned for an aide to open the car door so she could get back in.

He quickly moved across the street, opened the rear door on the other side, climbed in beside her, and smiled. "I know that this is unusual, Master Adept, and I ask for your forgiveness right here at the onset of our conversation." He didn't bother to try to shield his mind. If she wanted to look inside, he knew he'd not be able to stop her.

She nodded to him and said quite politely, "And to what do I owe this honor, Bram?"

He shuffled his feet on the car mat below his seat as he realized he was going to have to fully vocalize his issue today. Perhaps that was just the Master Adept's attempt to stop him before he began. So he began in a rush.

"Master Adept, I am, as of today, hereby resigning my station within the Issian faith. I wish to no longer be a part of the whole Issian way of life —and I'm sorry, Ma'am, but that is not negotiable ..." he finished off, his voice firm.

She just looked at him.

From what he could tell, as he searched his mind, there looking trying to look inside his head. Not a single thing.

She continued to just stare, one finger rubbing on the thumb of her right hand.

He went on. "Ma'am, so you know—I find myself at a place in my life, where I need to do things, to live life the way that I want—and that means that I can no longer be faithful to both the Issian way of life—and to myself. I ask, Master Adept, that you just let me go. With more than thousands of new Adept officers coming up via the naval academy, I do not think that I will be missed at all."

She shrugged as she said, "But a part of being an Adept officer is the skill and learning that comes along with experience—and you have had much of that, Bram."

He nodded but went on. "Master, I ask then that you let me go—I will make the solemn promise that all ex-Issians make to never, ever, use my powers for enrichment of myself but for others only. I so swear here and now."

He felt the reachings in his brain as the Master Adept leaned toward him and grasped his arm. With direct touch, one Issian cannot hide from another, and their two minds melded for a moment

—and then she let go.

She nodded to him, and on her face was the slightest of smiles. "You have chosen a very tough road to travel, Bram. But I—the whole of the Issian faith—wish you well. May you be successful in life —and in love," she said.

He nodded to her, and in moments, he stood outside the car as it pulled away.

"Guess she cut short her walkabout today," he said to himself.

"Guess I surprised her." He took a step back and turned.

"Guess I'm no longer an Adept officer in the Duchy Navy."

He walked slowly back along the sidewalk, and as the pedestrian traffic was slight, he made good time on his way out of the city center. Farther along the main street, he hailed a robo-cab and told it to take him to the Dessau Landing Port, so he could find a ride back to the Duchy d'Avigdor.

"One more person to tell this to ..." he said to himself, "my mentor ... the Duke d'Avigdor."

Each of the Leudies sat and nursed their own psyches as only Rulers can—neck snakes tightening around their necks. Eyes bugged out slightly as they—all thirty of them—were angry now about the report just tendered to the Leudie Trading Rules group, the council of thirty full trading members who ran the Leudie realm. Niels Lofton tried to find a way to swallow the news they'd just been given.

Around him at the huge round table, the rest of the Rulers sat, dressed in the usual Leudie black cloak with those dark green inserts. Some toyed with their tablets, others stroked their neck snakes to calm them, and a few even had doffed their toques and were spit polishing their badge of office, those three gold bars in a row.

"My neck snake is fine, my tablet I couldn't care less about, and my three bars are shiny," he said to himself.

But what was not fine was the report from the Leudie science ministry. The red power belts found on an inward-bound trip that held so much promise had an issue.

The science report stated plainly that nothing could pierce the force field generated by the simple red belt strapped around a wearer's waist. Nothing. No projectile, plasma bolt, energy weapon ray, or even a small tactical nuke could injure the person wearing the belt.

How it was powered was still beyond the reach of the science study so far. However, the force field around the wearer was a universal shield, which was the issue.

To hold off an enemy, one would turn on the belt and couldn't be injured at all. One could do almost anything. One could walk and swim and ride and fly about in a ship.

But what could not be done was to injure the person attacking you—unless the belt itself was turned off first.

This meant that an attacker could simply draw their weapon and wait while the wearer had the belt enabled. When the wearer tried to foist off the attacker, which meant turning off the belt, the attacker could then harm you.

Niels Lofton shook his head and sighed as he worked through and simplified the report's findings. The belt created a waiting game and locked the wearer and his attacker, whether man or machine, into a hold pattern. A simple robot weapon, aimed at you, could keep you at bay, waiting for you to turn off the belt and in milliseconds fire at you.

The findings in the report were not good. Every single Leudie at the table understood that, and every single Leudie realized the power belt had limitations.

One of the Rulers, a few seats to Lofton's right, spoke up. "So, I take it you've tested all weapons from within the power belt's interior? None work, right?"

That got a nod from the scientist in front of them.

"And I take it that until we understand more about the belts themselves, they are a simple defensive tool. No one wearing one can be hurt. But neither can they do any damage to any attackers around them—correct?"

The scientist once again just nodded.

"It was a letdown for sure," Niels said to himself, "yet surely just a defensive weapon would have some value, right?"

"Are there any more tests that you can think of—to try to get around this universal blocking?" another trader across the table questioned.

The scientist replied, "Well, yes, there are some more, of course—but we're having no luck no matter what we try. We even tried sending a live animal out—our test subjects held Garnuthian mice before activating the belt. Once the belt was activated, they threw the mice which simply hit the interior of the force field and fell to the floor. Still inside the belt's range and unhurt.

"Obviously, no living creature or any projectile or energy beam or light can leave the area being protected by the belt. Even a rockslide stops dead from crushing the belt wearer, suspended above the force field until the subject moves. Once the subject moves, the rockslide then falls to the ground. We are still investigating other items or means ... but as the report says, this may well be a simple defensive item that cannot be used in battle or conflict. At least not yet," he said.

Not a word was spoken from any of the Rulers. Each Leudie present, the top thirty traders on the planet, realized that perhaps their hopes were dashed.

But they all nodded, and the trader who was acting as the chairperson said, "We'll table that report, and let's move along. Item number eight today—the exclusionary exemptions on those new electronics from Roor. Trader Vidda, please ..."

"Got to think of something," Niels said to himself. "Surely there's a way to fix those belts ..."

Bouncing carefully across the bottom of the crater, Mel said to himself, "Working in airless space is, well, something that always makes me feel, well, less than efficient."

The *Exeter* had found the moon's asteroid after a hunt that involved going to the coordinates he'd been given—and then finding dozens more asteroids in that space.

Launching a shuttle, he'd had the helm put up a search grid, and they'd visited each one of them in turn, flying over and around each asteroid. Some were small at less than a few hundred yards across, but some were almost a mile wide. None, of course, was a sphere; all had lobes, valleys, and jutting crags that a meteorite could hide in. And each had to be looked at. Thank God for the eagle eyes on the *Exeter* science officer.

"Bingo, Captain," the lieutenant said, and he pointed at the screen.

On this asteroid, about halfway through the search grid, there was a valley that had craters from smaller meteor strikes from eons ago. At one end of the almost flat plain, a ridge of crags jutted up and into the blackness above. This body of asteroids was in a system that lay near the mid-point of Pentyaan space.

At approximately twenty lights wide and forty lights long, this space was claimed by the Pentyaan Oligarchy. The fact that the *Exeter* was even here, inside that space, was a serious offense. But they had come in from outside the normal flow of inbound traffic and had used a nebula just one system over to hide even more.

The *Exeter* sat in the nebula, clouded by the purple and green clouds of gas, and she was safe.

And the shuttle now lay just behind him on the relatively flat crater floor on the mile-long asteroid, as he bounced up the side of the crater and met the team involved with the mining of the ore. He'd been more than a bit perturbed when he'd received the mission documents from the Baroness just a week ago, which let him know the ore he was after could not be cut using lasers.

Somehow, lasers didn't work on that ore— something that was beyond his knowledge. The *Exeter* science officer had commented that just wasn't right—physics or some such thing had laws that can't be broken. But no matter, as the Baroness had also had huge band saws delivered to the *Exeter* that same day.

"Hard to use, yes," he said to himself as he watched the action fifteen feet below him in the mining pit.

Against an outcrop of the red ore from the tail end of the meteorite, they'd erected three scaffoldings around the thirty-foot-wide ore block. One of the crew stood up top, and around his waist, he had tied and supported the metal framework of the saw. Below him and off to either side, two more crew stood, and their jobs were to swing the saw from side to side from the focal point above, held by the man on top.

It was slow work, and it took almost a full two hours to saw off a piece that was about ten feet long and six feet wide. Each slice was only four inches thick, and while cumbersome to manage, other crew carted off the pieces. The pieces were stored in the shuttle for transport back to the *Exeter* later.

This was day three, and each day they'd been able to get about six slabs of ore. They had to switch crewmen since the air supply in their spacesuits was only good for three hours. "Still, the job was getting done, and that was a good thing," Mel said to himself. "Good indeed."

"Should get me some props from the Baroness," he said to himself as the next slab fell slowly as it was sawed free from the meteorite body. With almost zero gravity, the slab weighed next to nothing, and Magnusson stepped back and out of the way as support crew moved in to manhandle the latest slab back over the crater floor to the shuttle.

"At this rate," he said to himself, "we'll have, what, maybe ten tons of ore in the four days we figure we can hide out here without being found." The shuttle was on full dark and the only real lights being used were those fifteen feet down in the hole. They had almost no footprint on the asteroid.

Still, being found was a no-no, he knew. That would start some kind of diplomatic incident, and already the relations between the RIM Confederacy and the Pentyaan Oligarchy were poor. The latest rumors were that there was unrest on the rise here and talk even that one or two of the twenty-three realms that the Pentyaan Oligarchy controlled here were fighting for their independence.

Just the kind of rebellion that would be best to avoid, he thought and grinned as the crew manhandled the slab out of the hole and the cutting crew positioned the saw to begin on a new slab.

"Four more days," Mel said, but in his suit helmet, no one could hear him.

He smiled. In four days and a bit, the Baroness would receive his "mission complete and successful" EYES ONLY. *I wonder what might that be worth to my career ...* he thought, the grin still plastered on his face as he watched the next cut begin.

CHAPTER THREE

Up on the Ghayth space station, things were, as usual, slightly askew. In the last few minutes, three ships had come in, and each ship wanted landing permissions and of course, each wanted to go first. The *TN Crockett* from Tillion was making the most noise, as it was once again arguing that as an all-male ship, it would, of course, have precedence in landing order as those other two ships carried mixed gender crews.

At least that's what Captain McDonald, the duty officer up on the station bridge got from the rant that the Tillion captain had just spewed at him via Ansible. He shook his head. Tillions were uni-gendered it was assumed. A few months back, a video had been released showing why that was, and Tillion had issued a public denial stating the video was fraudulent. Captain McDonald, like most RIM citizens, had not been swayed by the Tillion claims. He smiled to himself and decided one of the other ships should be allowed in first, and as he was the duty officer, that choice was his.

"Ansible, contact the Thrones freighter. Allow them to go down first. Pad number twenty-one is for them. Don't notify the others, just let them sit," he said.

That ought to pay back the Tillions for their uni-gender stance, he thought.

The Thrones freighter yawed to its port side and then began the long glide down toward the Ghayth landing port. The Ansible notice up on the station view-screen flashed as the Tillion ship asked for recognition.

Captain McDonald chose to ignore it and said, "Blame it on the newness of the systems here on the station," to the Ansible station.

The sergeant who manned the Ansible console on the bridge nodded. New to Ghayth, the space station had been in service less than a month; as always, one could expect some shortfalls in how things worked and at what speed too.

The sergeant spoke into his throat mic to the other two ships, and they all watched as the Thrones freighter became smaller and smaller as it dropped down on its aft side to land a hundred miles below.

"Normal station stuff," the captain said to himself, and then he nodded to the sergeant to send the Tillions down next. He placed them on landing pad twenty-four—well enough away from the Thrones ship to make them happy. The last ship was the RIM Confederacy frigate the *RN Henderson*, who had the duty this month of making Confederacy deliveries around the whole RIM.

"Barony Drive has made the duty of mail run easier for the *Henderson*," the sergeant said as he finished up with the final landing permissions and instructions for the RIM Navy ship, and the lieutenant smiled.

"It has done that, but as we're learning—while the time between planets has shrunk to seconds—it also has made redundant the long-range scans. By the time we get a notice that a ship is approaching, it's here. No prior notice means that three arrive at once like today—and that might be problematic sometime in the future ..." he said as he sipped his coffee.

With Ghayth lying just at the far edge of the RIM Confederacy space, all alone in the immediate area, the duty on board the *Wilson* was a solitary type of duty. Yes, the planet below with almost a hundred thousand new immigrants was well worth the shore leave, but overall, McDonald knew that being captain of the *Wilson* was much like babysitting. "Not much happens, not many care, and for the most part, the station would be a simple portal down to the planet. Easy duty," he said and snorted to himself. "Pretty much a boring job."

Not that navy jobs were all boring, he did rationalize to himself, like the three ships showing up with no prior notice.

Navy men all over the RIM had commented on that already, and he knew it had been discussed at the Barony Captains Council too. He'd been at that Captains Council meeting just a month back, when this brand new Ghayth space station, the *BN Wilson*, was being barged into place.

He smiled. With the recent loss of the admiral—as Higgins had left the Barony Navy to join the new duke and the Duchy d'Avigdor Navy, someone had to replace him. And the Baroness had left it to the Captains Council to promote from within.

Four ballots it had taken, but the new admiral of the Barony Navy was Eleanor Vennamo. She would move up from being captain of the *Gibraltar* to now being in charge of the whole Barony Navy. That had made—or so the scuttlebutt had said—the Baroness very happy. He wondered how it might have been received on Tillion, but that was for another time and place.

He knew Vennamo; he'd been an ensign on the *Gibraltar* himself more than five years ago. He'd learned she was a fair but strict captain. She had been meager in her praise and expected all to perform at their best levels. He had tried but fallen short a few times and had heard about it in spades. Still, as admiral, she'd be the kind of boss who would make the captains toe the Barony line—that he did know. And that she'd kept the *Gibraltar* as her flagship came as no surprise either—that destroyer was home base for her. Sometimes, he did miss the ship.

He stretched and for the umpteenth time, he wondered who'd be coming in next and what kind of—

Klaxons screamed around him as a ship popped up right in front of the space station.

His eyes widened as he took in how enormous the ship was. Not from the RIM was his next thought. He yelled at the sergeant to kill the sirens around them, and the bridge lapsed into silence.

He was thankful for the silence. This ship did not carry the required ID of a RIM Confederacy ship in the *Wilson's* database. Therefore, it was an intruder—and he began to bark out orders.

"Ansible, notify Commander Williams we've got company; Helm, turn her slightly to port so we can get a good look at her; notify Major Stal we've got a situation here as well ..." he said quickly, and as the space station turned to port about twenty degrees, he took a better look.

"She was big all right," he said to himself. The ship looked to be more than a mile long and tubular in shape. Towers pointed out the top end and the bottom too, which meant there was no aft end with engines. How she flew, he had no quick guess. In the center of that mile-long tube, a round disk about seven hundred feet in height and at least two thousand feet in width was wrapped around the axis of the ship. He could see—if he was right— landing bays lit up and windows or portholes with light streaming out from the interior. He had no idea if his guesses were correct as he was using human standards.

He jammed his thumb down on the console beside him, forcing the Ansible into an EYES ONLY emergency request to speak to the Baroness. It was not accepted for whatever reason, but he got a secondary message through to the RIM Navy admiral. He reported what he could see and added that the ship had appeared only. It was doing nothing aggressive at all.

It sat there, a hundred miles above Ghayth, and was doing nothing. Captain McDonald watched the ship for any activity, and time slowly passed.

The captain sat up straighter when an odd light

caught his eye. A beam—narrow and laser-like, the *Wilson* AI displayed in the view-screen sidebar, shot out at the station glowing in an ultra-bright teal shade. It touched the *Wilson* for a second or two and then went out.

"Maybe that's their communications," his Ansible sergeant said, "but I got nothing."

He nodded at the sergeant who was looking back at him and said, "Yes, give them a hail."

They waited as the view-screen showed in the sidebar that such a message had been sent.

There was no answer. The flashing message sent icon continued to flash.

He waited and thought about what to do next, but he knew he was to take no actions that in any way could be deemed as being aggressive at all.

"We sit and we wait," he said.

The Ansible was busy as incoming messages were being received, and the next hour was spent in repeating over and over that there was no reason at this point to feel threatened. The alien ship just hung above the planet doing nothing.

"Can we perhaps probe inside the ship?" he asked his science officer who had just been found on the station and had hustled up to the bridge.

"Don't know. Most of our scans that I see show no ship there at all. Every single one—thermal, particle, mass, photonic—not a single register on any of the scopes. They are not there, Captain.

"Course, the infrared can't lie. There is a mass there that is radiating heat—it's what the station scanner saw, and that prompted the klaxons to go off. Ships radiate heat into space, so yes, it's a ship, but no, we can't scan it for anything else, sir."

He sounded as frustrated as the rest of them.

Captain McDonald grunted. "No matter that our eyes say there is a ship there, the station sees it as a mass since the ship doesn't have a Confederacy ID ... so we can't find out more. Great." McDonald sighed. "Report that back to all parties too, Ansible," he said, and they sat back to await whatever might come next.

Helena looked over at him and her face was like a mask. Tanner couldn't tell what she was thinking, and for the millionth time, he wished he could have been an Issian so he could read her mind and know what kind of answer to give.

In his office on the third floor of the duchy palace, he reached forward and picked up his drink. "Well, not really a drink per se—more of a liquid refreshment," he said to himself.

Cured of his alcoholism years ago, via the Revia vaccine administered by his medical team on the Barony Hospital Ship, he could drink any alcoholic beverage without any effects. But he no longer liked the taste of scotch at all. Wine was okay; the taste, flavors, and bouquet were all fun to learn and to teach to his taste buds like all new wine drinkers knew.

This was different. This liqueur had come by his way at a state dinner just a few weeks back. They'd been celebrating the signing of a new trade deal between the Duchy d'Avigdor and Merilda, and the earl had been his guest at the dinner. From Merilda, he had brought a case of their own local signature libation—it was called Hanka, and it was made, the earl had said, from honey bees that had only used the flowers of a certain wildflower to make that honey. Mead he might have called it, but Hanka was its name. And he liked it.

He sipped a little from the tall straight-sided highball glass and knew he had to speak. "I want you to know that this was the toughest decision I've ever had to face," he said to his wife.

Helena just nodded. No help there.

"I have made my decision known to the chief justice—and yes, some might call that 'judicial interference,' which is both correct—and irrelevant. It is my decision—"

Helena butted in. "No, darling—it is your decision. You were the one that was almost a victim, and two others at our wedding were not so lucky. So whatever you decide is more than fine with me. Allow me to watch with you, and I'll learn like all the rest of the RIM will," she said.

She had said it nicely. No real antagonism or put-down or bullying either in her voice. She meant it, and that made him love her even more.

He nodded and on the view-screen on the wall, suddenly they were watching the courtroom across the city and Gia's trial was on the screen.

They'd been watching now for almost a week, with all of the jockeying of positions for the prosecution and the defense team before the trial even began. They'd watched as the defense had chosen a bench trial instead of a jury trial. That meant the judge, or the three judges as in this case, would be the finders of fact and the ruler on matters of law and procedure. The judges would decide the credibility of the evidence presented at trial; the judges would also decide what happened at the trial according to laws and rules of procedure. This was a good thing, Tanner knew, and he'd counted on it.

With the vids—many with different angles and full sound audio of the attack at the wedding and the murders of the Master Adept and Duke David d'Avigdor—seen now for more than a year, there was little chance of finding a jury pool that was un-tainted by those vids. Even today, they were playing out all over the airwaves, with shot-by-shot color commentary by announcers all over the RIM.

After the bench trial had been decided upon, the defense moved on to evidence and the whole question of the videos themselves was the first hurdle. The defense attorney had even asked the three superior court judges if they had seen same, and they had acknowledged that, like the rest of the RIM citizens, they had seen the videos.

Once that had been established, the defense filed their motion that the vids should not be allowed into evidence in Gia's trial, as they were already an established prejudicial part of the case against her. That had been hard-fought by the prosecution; the arguments for and against had taken a whole morning. The defense had lost on that motion, and the vids were prominently displayed and run both in real speed and in slow motion.

Tanner had not watched that only yesterday, choosing to leave the office and to return when Helena had come to get him from the hallway outside.

Earlier today, the medical team from the Barony Hospital Ship who had been assigned to diagnose Gia had presented the medical evidence. Doctor Etter had taken the stand as the defendant's psychiatrist. After his oath, he had sat, and Tanner had paid particular attention to the doctor's testimony.

Gia's attorney, Alpert, began with a run-through of the doctor's credentials, which the prosecution immediately stood up to agree that the doctor was an expert in his field. With that out of the way, Alpert began to slowly go through the eleven months of Gia's time up on the Barony Hospital Ship and what the doctor had reported as to his early, interim, and late diagnoses of her psyche.

Doctor Etter was, Tanner thought, a consummate doctor, and he presented with the correct and perfect blend of clinician and yet a human being too. Gia, he stated, had been what he would call 'brainwashed' into believing that her sister Nora had been killed by her brother, Duke Tanner Scott. That, the doctor went on to say, had been disproved by the tribunal that had tried the duke decades ago —he'd been found not guilty of that. But Gia's mother had used every means available to imprint on Gia, her remaining daughter, that in fact it had been Tanner's fault.

"That had put Gia squarely in the middle of a contest of loyalty, a contest which cannot possibly be won between her mother and her brother ..." Doctor Etter finished off.

"And what could that have done to lead to the wedding day attacks?" Alpert asked.

Doctor Etter nodded. "What that meant was that

with the hatred for Tanner, built up daily by the growing up in the home and the daily attributions of Nora's death laid at Tanner's feet, Gia was delusional. That's our official medical diagnosis, she was not of sound mind when the attacks occurred. And, it was that delusional indoctrination that we eventually were able to get Gia to see was untrue just recently. She is sane—now. And, yes, there will be consequences for her crimes, but all mitigated by her delusional state at the time. At least that's our opinion."

"Objection, Your Honor. This opinion is not medical evidence but, instead, judicial opinion," the prosecution stood and said dryly.

"Objection sustained," the head judge said.

The defense counsel said, "Your witness."

The prosecution smiled at the doctor. "Just a few questions, Doctor. Was it not you who treated the brother—Tanner Scott—when he was sent to the Barony Hospital Ship a few years back for a ninety-day sanity test?"

"It was, and I can report that we found that patient sane and compos mentis, as you lawyers say," Doctor Etter replied with syrup on his voice.

"Yes, thank you, Doctor. So you're familiar with the brother—the current Duke d'Avigdor—and his own mental state, are you not, having been his own psychiatrist?" the prosecution went on.

"I am—but with full patient confidentiality, I cannot discuss that here," Etter said smugly.

"Nonsense, Doctor. You and I and the court knows, that as you've opened the door by offering up medical diagnosis on Gia by using the duke and his innocence, you can no longer use that shield here. So I ask, Doctor—do you have any knowledge of the state of the duke's own mind when it comes to the death of Nora?"

Etter looked over at the defense counsel, but Alpert sat immobile. He looked up at the judge next, but the judge said, "You will answer the question, Doctor, as asked."

Doctor Etter shook his head but spoke anyways. "Yes, I do have that information."

"Doctor, the judge directed you to answer the question," the prosecution said.

Doctor Etter sighed. "The judge said to answer the question as it was asked. You asked if I had any knowledge of the state of the duke's mind—"

"And would you share that knowledge here, please, as evidence?" the prosecutor asked.

Doctor Etter grimaced but did answer. "Tanner—the duke—was of the opinion that he was innocent of the murder of Nora. Yet, he had his doubts and said that it often was in his dreams ... that he had somehow killed her. But, and I repeat this as a medical fact, many, many patients have these kind of dreams with culpability issues—when in fact there were none. Again, he was found innocent in the tribunal ..."

"But perhaps not so innocent within his own mind?" the prosecution said as he left the lectern to return to his seat.

"Objection, Your Honor—assumes facts not in evidence!" Alpert just about shouted as he jumped to his feet.

"Sustained. Clerk, strike that from the record," the judge said and the room was abuzz with mutterings out in the visitors' gallery.

Tanner took another sip of the Hanka, wishing he could get a buzz that would help him stave off his growing headache. Still, he knew there would be more to come, and he looked over at Helena. She was watching from the big wing chair positioned at the side of his desk, and she'd turned the chair around to face the view-screen. She leaned over, patted him on the arm, and said, "Never mind, honey, doctors are removed from the rest of us," and he smiled at that.

The trial, of course, went on. The defense, led by Alpert, was pretty good, he thought, and Alpert called more witnesses too. He called the clerk who'd issued the press credentials to Gia that showed she was an accredited member of the press, attending the wedding as a Gallipedia reporter.

Alpert used that to show Gia was impersonating a member of the press and taking advantage of her employment with Gallipedia. Even though Gia was a Gallipedia member, she was listed on her employment registry as being on sabbatical at the time of the wedding and not on any work-related assignments for Gallipedia.

Several press members spoke of her standoffish personality, which Alpert implied meant she was in some kind of state where she was not acting "normal."

The prosecution objected profusely with each witness, and yet Alpert went on.

He called the head of the EliteGuards who was on duty that day. He testified that when they'd tackled Gia, she was acting crazy. She was crying but screaming that she just needed one more photo of her brother ... just one more, as she fought to keep her camera in her hands. The guard knew, as they all did, that the camera was also a weapon. He'd covered it with his torso as he dove on Gia and had wrestled it out of her hands almost immediately.

Again, the prosecution objected. This time, it was that the term "crazy" was a medical term, which was outside the guard's realm of expertise. Alpert argued that as a guard for Royalty, they were all trained to recognize oddball behavior around their protected charges. The judge agreed and let that testimony stand.

Alpert finished calling his witnesses.

All in all the prosecution had presented only the videos. They had played and showed Gia shooting the Master Adept and Duke David d'Avigdor who had died as well as Tanner who had survived. Then they had rested.

The defense had presented the medical testimony as fact. The defense presented a handful of witnesses who had contact with the defendant just before the killings and could testify that Gia's behaviors and actions showed she was not of sound mind when the attack had occurred.

The prosecution had an easy time, Tanner saw, of making their closing statement. They simply, once again, played the video.

The defense lawyer, Alpert, rose. In his ten-minute summation and closing, he leaned on the fact that the best medical team that could be found in the Barony had diagnosed the defendant as being delusional—a product of her maternal brainwashing as to the establishment of blame for her sister's death placed on her brother, Tanner.

And since that time more than a year ago, great strides had been made. The defendant no longer was non compos mentis—she knew that her mother had placed her in an indefensible position. But that had all changed.

"In closing, she is innocent now," Alpert said, "no matter how guilty she was then ..." and he sat.

Tanner wondered about everything that had been presented and said, but as a non-legal type, he wasn't quite sure as to what had been said in a legal sense.

The judges thanked the two teams of lawyers in front of them and remanded the court for their deliberations. As they rose to leave the room, the camera providing the feed for his viewing spun around to show the visitors standing as the judges left. In the front row stood Bram.

That was a surprise to Tanner and Helena, but she spoke up first. "Bram ... that's Bram right there," she said as she pointed.

Tanner grunted in reply at first.

"Wonder why he'd be there," she asked.

Tanner shook his head. "No idea, but judging by the look on his face, it meant something to him," he replied.

On Bram's face was a look that Tanner had never seen before—one of wonder yet anxious wonder. Surely, he had looked around in the minds in the courtroom and found out all he'd need to know.

"Judging by what I just saw," Helena said, "I think that she will be found guilty but with mitigating circumstances. Her sentence will likely be very lenient," she said.

Tanner looked away from Bram to her and said, "I agree."

She nodded and they turned back to watch Bram as he left the camera's range, and the courtroom emptied.

"AI," Tanner said, "find Ayla, please, and send her in."

Moments later, his new lieutenant commander came in with her gold oak leaf collar devices shining brightly.

"Ayla—couple of things if I can," he said, and she nodded, tablet poised to take down his requests.

"First, find Bram for me and have him in here sometime, say, tomorrow," he began as she typed.

"Next, do a search here on the RIM for liqueurs similar to this Hanka from Merilda. Would like to try others if there are any such ones available."

She grinned at him at that one but said not a word as she typed.

"Then there's our 'do not disturb' status—you may unlock that as of, say, tomorrow earliest, please, I've been away from the world now for two days, and that's enough. Good?" he asked.

She nodded. "Aye, Your Grace. Will do," she said, and she turned to leave his office as quickly as she had arrived.

Helena smiled. "She's a real find. Makes me

want to go to Hope and ask if they'd like to join the Duchy d'Avigdor," she said as she sipped her glass of Hanka.

"Not a chance—they're far and away too much of an individual type only kind of planet," he said.

"So," Helena said as she twisted in the big wing chair and swung her feet up and underneath her as she snuggled into the deep upholstery, "about how long will the deliberations take?"

He shrugged. "Long enough I suspect," he said with some small degree of a smile, "to let the three judges come to agreement.

"Fine. Then let's think about, say, a weekend away once this is over. Bottle maybe?" she asked.

He grinned at her and shook his head. "How about a great hunting trip to Anulet?"

She groaned as he told her about the upcoming treat he'd arranged for his groomsmen, and their talks continued into early evening.

#####

"Being young is a good thing," he said to himself. Young, eager, enthusiastic, ambitious—all worked for him. If there was one thing Captain Magnusson knew about himself, it was that he was going to be an admiral one day. One day soon.

After all, hadn't he completed, with great aplomb, that secret mission for the Baroness just a month or so ago?

If that meant he was willing to risk his ship and his crew at times, then that was something he'd consider at the time. Until now—other than the recent spate of testing for the Barony Drive—he'd always played it by the book, as they said.

Out of the Eons Academy almost ten years ago, he had worked his way up the command structure on the *Sterling* under Captain Flannery, who had given him the XO's job almost seven years ago.

Now, he was a full-fledged captain on the *BN Exeter*, and he was happy with that—for now.

"But one day ..." he said to himself as he nodded to the helm, and the *Exeter* followed the space station's directions and docked off landing bay number three. He smiled at the helmsman. "Jefferson, you've got hands of magic, lad," he said, and he did mean it.

Finding an exact spot in space with no real markers—curbs, bumpers, or docks—to land up against took a skill this helmsman had in spades. From here, it'd be a two-minute ride in the *Exeter's* shuttle over to the landing bay, and that was a perk that came from having great crewmen. Or in this case, a great crewwoman, as Jefferson was a tall Farthian alien—slightly thicker than one might think through the torso and waist and supported on long legs that were always within boots. Her head was almost torpedo shaped, but with her large eyes and the overlapping ocular range, she could see exceptionally well, which was another reason that having a Farthian at the helm was the gold standard.

She nodded to her captain and said, "Aye, Sir ... but the *Exeter* is such an easy craft to handle."

He nodded and picked up the bag from beside the captain's chair on the bridge. Hoisting the bag over a shoulder, he grinned at the weight and the slight clinking from within.

As he walked, he went over the recent EYES ONLY he'd just had a day ago with the Baroness. Working for her meant that the admiral—the new one, Vennamo—must know too. After all, taking a full frigate out of the normal flow of shifts and missions and duties must be noticeable to navy headquarters—and Vennamo was one for the books. She supposedly had an eye on everything under her in the Barony Navy except the *Exeter* and him. For at least the hundredth time this week, he grinned and said to himself, "How good it is to have a Royal in your corner."

His next task was to resolve an issue with the gypsies. Magnusson would have to use his selling skills—the best ones he had—to get the gypsies to buy in. The Baroness had spelled that out to him, and he had agreed—as he knew he would—and had told her not to worry, he'd sell the deal to the refugees, no problem.

He trooped out and off the bridge after giving the comm to his science officer as he went to the lift to take a down car to the shuttles on Deck Two and was soon jetting over to the station. After docking in the huge landing bay, he went to the station center and up the escalator to the third level. He went down another long corridor that swung slowly to the left as it curved around the station, and moments later, he was at the doorway to a conference room the Baroness had provided for his use.

Two people sat at the table in the center of the room. Captain Daika Rossum sat at one spot, and beside her, her husband, who was also her her chief mate, Guari glowered at him. *Husband and wife,* he thought and shook his head, but that was how they did things in the Vitsa of Iron—a Roma family group of metalworkers, who had come to the Barony as refugees.

In fact, these gypsies had provided the single item that had helped the RIM Confederacy defeat the aliens that had come to the RIM via their ship, the *Scavenger*. The gypsies had stolen that ship from the aliens years earlier, and since it was still recognized by the aliens as a part of their own reaper ships, the RIM Task Force had been able to destroy the invaders.

On Memories, Magnusson remembered, a full frigate from the RIM Navy fleet, the *BN Jamison*, had been gifted to these two in trade as the RIM had needed to use their ship.

That had led, via several odd occurrences, to their lab samples being held for further testing, which now had been done by the Barony science ministry —rather than the Roma crew themselves. And the sample of the red metal ore had started all of this.

"Which had led," Captain Magnusson said to himself, "to me."

He smiled as he sat down and thanked them for coming to meet with him. Niceties followed and they all were aware the meeting had not yet been started—this was just for social graces.

He reached down, picked up his bag, and placed it on the table. "Do you remember the time when, from the *Scavenger*, all of your items were removed so we could use as much space as we could to hold ordnance in the fight against the invaders on Memories?" he began.

They nodded. The man, the chief mate, leaned forward to speak, but his wife, the captain, motioned him to keep silent.

"A part of that huge movement of items included the removal, and storage for you, of some small pallets and cases of ore samples from the labs you kept up on the second level — remember?" he continued.

They both nodded again.

"One of those samples, this one," he said as he reached into the bag, took out a chunk of the ore, and plopped it on the table where it landed with a clunk, "Xithricite, I'm told it's called, was found in a box of other samples."

They nodded again but again said nothing, so he went on.

"It was labeled properly, and as we noted, it came from off the RIM — outside our boundaries. I just happened to be stationed on the duty desk over at the Barony naval hall when the request from our labs came in. I knew right away what it meant to the Barony to have access to this ore, and I took it upon myself to look into the location where the ore had come from ..."

This was the cover story the Baroness and he had cooked up to keep the real import of the mission a secret.

Still not a word from the two across the table.

"The asteroid's coordinates were easily found, and the *Exeter* took a quick trip. We found what you found — a no-name asteroid field, circling the planet, along with others. Some kind of collision had obviously occurred with the planet's moon perhaps, and the moon's asteroids were plentiful and mostly spread out around the planet still in orbit around same.

"In that system, the only planet that lay in the Cinderella zone was empty of sentient life ... with little to make it a new colony except for birds maybe. High, high mountain ranges, long slow slopes down to heavily salted seas. No people or aliens. Little life on the ground, but yes, lots of colorful avian life.

"You'll love this. Our shuttle landed near a beautiful lake somewhere on one continent, and in five minutes, we were surrounded with birds—but birds that instead of having legs and talons or feet— had a ball that they rolled around on. Talk about weird." Captain Magnusson shook his head

Captain Magnusson picked up the chunk of Xithricite and tossed it back and forth from his right hand to his left hand. The gypsy captain and her husband kept their eyes on the Xithricite but still showed no reaction or signs of speaking.

The captain sighed and continued with his story. "But it was the asteroid that we were interested in. We searched and found it. We saw the huge impact site on a side of the asteroid where there was a flat plain and then a rising ride of crags. The red metal meteorite hit, plowed down through those crags, and buried itself deep within. But the tail end of that meteorite was visible—we could see where someone, perhaps from the *Scavenger*, had helped themselves to a small sample, and it was there that we began to mine the red metal ore. Only we didn't throw them into a box, we took them back to the *Exeter* for a full analysis."

The captain, Daika, leaned forward. "Interesting, we suppose, Captain. But so what?"

"This is the red ore that the planet Enki—a part of the Caliphate—mines in huge quantities. It may come as a shock to you, but this ore, when smelted and refined, makes whatever it shields invulnerable to all space weapons. No plasma, laser, energy cannon can pierce the metal plates ..." he said.

The chief mate struggled to free his arm from the iron grip of his wife as he spoke up. "While that is something we did not know, it should belong to us —the Vitsa of Iron, our clan. You would never have found it without us!" he almost shouted.

Magnusson nodded in agreement and went on. "Yes, that is true. But in any case, we were able to take only so much of the ore. We smelted it rather poorly but did make these testing samples for a start," he said. He reached into his bag and pulled out sheets of red metal about twenty inches long by ten inches wide. "We've tested these, and they are, without a doubt, Xithricite. Covering a ship with these would make it invulnerable to enemy fire— but not projectiles. It has no value for that kind of defense, but for spaceships, they do not use projectile cannons and the like. At least not yet," he said.

"And why do you tell us this, as it appears that you believe you own this ore and the resulting fortunes that will be made from same," the chief mate said, his voice dripping with irony.

Magnusson nodded. "Here's the issue and why I've brought you into this. I'm way past what I can do to help anymore with this kind of undercover discovery. I need—the Barony needs—help on this, so I am going to ask you for help. After all, it's your discovery originally, is it not?"

That got two nods from across the table.

"So, here's what has to happen. You go back to this bird planet system and the asteroid; mine ore and fill up the cargo holds on your ship, bringing the ore here to Neres. I will go to the Baroness and get this plan approved, and that will allow us to accept the ore, smelt it, and forge new armor for our fleet. You will reap whatever benefits might accrue from same. You win. And the Barony wins ..." he said smoothly.

"As do you," Daika said, her eyes never leaving his. She sat with her back rigid on the chair. She was not happy with his proposition, but it was going to be accepted.

He smiled at her as he fingered the red plates of

metal on the tabletop. "This is good for everyone, the Vitsa of Iron as well as the Barony, yes?"

They looked at him for a second or two, and then they both used their fingertips to touch the hammer and cogs icon on their vests at the same time, signifying they agreed.

He smiled on the escalator ride down to the landing bay level and thought this had gone well. They'd mine the ore, he knew, and that would free the RIM Confederacy from any kind of Pentyaan blame.

These were refugees—scavenging gypsies—with no real standing here on the RIM.

The ride up to full admiral doesn't appear to be so hard, he thought as he almost hummed right out loud.

Admiral McQueen slammed his hand down on the table in front of him, and the room was startled into silence. They were all piled into the anteroom to the admiral's suite of offices on Juno. Navy men and women from all over the RIM Confederacy perched on sofas and divans or sat on office chairs raided from the inside offices. Some even stood against the big windows, a hip leaning on the windowsill.

The room was full of other admirals and even some heads of state, which was perhaps why the silence ensued, but McQueen broke that silence right away.

"Pardon me for my no-nonsense approach, but we need to work on our plans and come up with answers as soon as possible," he said.

"Why might that be—this issue of urgency, Admiral. This alien ship has hung over Ghayth now for almost, what, ten days, and nothing has happened," Barony Admiral Vennamo asked.

She was right, but something was up with that ship, and McQueen knew they needed to act now. "Admiral, this is aggression of a type we have not faced—all of you know that. But the fact that they are doing nothing is not the point—they are in our space, and we need to have something to say about it."

An admiral in the uniform of the Hope navy spoke up. "Correct me if I'm wrong on this, please, but as I understand the position of this planet, Ghayth—it is outside the boundary limits of the RIM Confederacy," she said as she held up a hand to go on without interruption. "Yes, those buoys will be moved over to include the Valissian system but only when Ghayth is officially a part of the Barony, yes?"

That got nods around the table.

Tanner spoke up then, figuring that maybe a Royal might help. "I shouldn't have to remind any of you of the recent invasion by those reaper aliens on Memories just a few years back. That too was not a part of the RIM, but I don't think that any of us would think that they would disappear after they mined Memories for resources. We were going to be next, so in this case, I'd plead the same kind of thinking. We need, as Admiral McQueen noted, to make up a task force with the authority to protect the RIM Confederacy and that we need to do today —right here and right now," he said.

Some knocked on the table while others knocked on the walls. The knocking was deafening with so many crowded into the anteroom to the admiral's office.

McQueen nodded. He continued with the stats about the aliens. At this time, they had yet to learn much about the potential enemy. "So far, in ten days, we have hailed them hundreds of times. No answer.

"We have sent over a shuttle three times, I believe, and they get about a mile or so off the alien landing bay doors and hit the alien force field.

"We have sent a probe that also cannot get past the force field either.

"We are monitoring their ship, but we see nothing—no communications, no Ansible—nothing to show that there is even anyone home.

"It hangs there, does nothing, but does show a posture that we can imagine might turn adversarial, so I ask that we, here today, work out the details of a task force to go and stand off their front door, waiting. Waiting but poised to take full attack action should that present itself.

That got some more knocks, and the Ttseen admiral in the room howled his agreement.

"If I may," Admiral Vennamo said, "would it be agreeable to the group if we—the Barony—took on the leadership position as the head of the new task force? Guess that would be me on the *Gibraltar*. We'd like, too, for there to be a heavy showing of firepower at our side too," she said.

McQueen nodded, and in the next ten minutes, plans had been laid for the new task force.

There would be sixteen ships from navies all across the RIM Confederacy. As well, the RIM Navy would send four more to add up to a twenty-ship task force all due to assemble above Ghayth in two days. Should there be a change to current circumstances, then that would need to be sped up to handle whatever had occurred.

Admiral Vennamo would be the task force leader, and her ship, the *Gibraltar*, would be the flagship.

Tanner smiled and knew that Admiral Higgins

would be chafing under the much younger task force leader, but that was to be expected.

"Reminder. These aliens have what looks like superior technology—just try to scan their ship, and you'll see what I mean. As well, we are to remember that aggression comes in many forms—and these are aliens to us at this point, so judge your actions accordingly."

That got nods around the room too.

McQueen stood off the edge of the wide seat on the windowsill and smiled at them, but it was a very small smile. "Good luck—I'd like to be kept in the loop, Admiral" he said to the task force leader.

Vennamo smiled at him. "Always, Admiral, always ..."

The hastily arranged meeting broke up as the task force members went home to arrange for their new commitments.

CHAPTER FOUR

On the *Wisp*, the Praix were on downtime. Their ship sat over a planet that was not theirs nor was this even their own galaxy. They knew they were intruders, interlopers and—perhaps in the eyes of the planet—maybe even invaders. But that didn't matter. All of the Praix were still on downtime, and none prepared for any type of defensive maneuvers.

The Praix believed they had nothing to worry about. The inhabitants here—in fact all across this galaxy—were inferior when it came to technology and more. So downtime had been the caw that had gone out to the crew.

With less than a hundred souls in crew, the captain had just closed his eyes and thought the message to them all at once. A much larger ship, with hundreds of crew, might have needed a proxy re-send, where the captain spoke to some while his bridge crew spoke to others, and the message got to them all that way.

"But the *Wisp* is small," the captain said to himself as he shuffled his feet on the captain's perch on the bridge, shifting his weight at the same time. He flexed his wing tips, smoothing out the light feathers at the tip with his beak and his alula as his carpus fingers all stretched and flexed at the same time. Usually, a Praix would use his beak to choose a button to push or a door to open, but they all had the rudiments of a hand like the other lesser races did.

This waiting was getting on his nerves. He hopped over to look down at the console screen on his station and noted most of the crew was either in their quarters or in the central aviary, where a Praix could fly full tilt for over a thousand feet. Stretching the wings was good, he knew. Kept a Praix sane, he'd always thought.

The console showed that the ship's cook and his cooking flock were in the kitchen. He wondered what might be rustled up for the evening meal, hoping that once again it might be something good. Frozen rations were fine, and yet the supplementing of real fresh live kill was so, so much better. He sighed—at least as much as any

Praix could sigh—and said to himself, "No sense in getting your heart set on something that wasn't possible."

They were here, off Ghayth, waiting. They waited for the welcome that was obviously on its way.

The Praix captain knew a few ships lay around them as well as a small space station. The engineering flock leader, who admitted that she was just guessing, had identified the larger object as a space station.

Each time a ship had appeared, an ultra-bright teal ray had gone out to touch that ship for a second or two, registering that ship with the Praix engineering flock database. They did that for all the ships that were near them.

"Low-tech race, no real technology at all, rudimentary weapons and power sources, and ships without any real kind of shields either," the engineering flock leader had pronounced. "Bi-peds, warm blooded, two sexes—much like the race of our slaves, the Issians, to a degree.

"Short lives with no real high-stress capabilities. Use language—both written and spoken. No real minds with any degree of strength either. We did find three Issians—but all are low-grade barely competent minds. That is the big disappointment, but we did note that word of our entry to their system has been made all across this tiny realm. So we wait, for their allegiance oath givers."

She ruffled her feathers as she added, "We did, however, send out a galaxy-wide message to all Issians that we have arrived. We got no response as yet either, which is odd, but we will determine more at a later date," she said.

The morale flock had prepared an evening's entertainment for the ship's crew. *"We will be looking at streams from the Bootes Galaxy and what the recent flood of our ships encountered."*

Interesting content they've touted this as, the captain saw in his mind as the mind message came in. *Might find the time to fly over to that,* he thought as he stretched his wings out fully. Ten feet across, they were fully feathered, and the shine on the dorsal feathers was bright and sleek.

He clicked his beak, the click loud here on the bridge, but he was alone. No one heard his laughter.

This was about the easiest duty he'd ever had, yet he was still perturbed. The *Wisp* was a secondary Praix ship, and here he was in a galaxy the race had not even made into one of their own. He had friends who'd taken big cruisers and those huge consort ships to other destinations, but not him. He'd been relegated to this secondary ship to a third-world galaxy.

He snapped his beak, and the loud report echoed on the bridge. *Food first,* he thought. *Then off to the aviary where I can softly fly and glide as the stream from Bootes is shown. Then maybe perch time.*

He took one more look at the space around the *Wisp,* and there was nothing new there. Same ships and the same station, and while he didn't bother, he knew he could have drilled down to look inside the ships, but that was being monitored by the Praix database AI. There was nothing to fear from these aliens. They just were not capable of being a threat and would, he knew, have made—might still make —a great new subservient race for the Praix as their first conquest of this galaxy.

#####

Anulet was a world like few others, Tanner knew. The *Sword* dropped back into real space from the Barony Drive, and the ship was in high orbit for a few minutes.

Anulet was a small planet of only about five thousand miles in diameter. All humans would be working against much less gravity here than on other planets of larger size. This would allow them to feel much stronger, have more endurance, and, of course, be able to take long bounding strides of almost twelve feet at a full run. But the gravity wasn't what was so different.

111

The planet's double suns were what made it such an oddball. Anulet was the fourth planet of one of the binary stars, a red giant, named Oz by earlier colonists on Anulet. Being a red giant, the light that fell on Anulet for the most part was reddish light, which deepened the shadows and made contrasting shades that could hurt your eyes to some degree after exposure for a few days. Of course, the colonists had become inured to that a few generations back, and all Anuletians paid the problem no attention.

Oz was not the only sun that shone down on the planet. Eons ago, Oz had captured a smaller main sequence star called Wizard, and with its yellowish light, the shadows on Anulet were often muddy, deep in brownish tones. Every four years, the paths of the suns lined up to shine on Anulet. Right now, only Oz shone down on the planet as Wizard was eclipsed. All shadows would be a deep red color, and the contrasts would be bright for months to come. The light and shadows were only a bit different from when he'd been here before hunting for Jaels.

The *Sword* received notice to proceed to land on the landing pad at the main lodge buildings a few thousand miles below. Lieutenant Cooper spun the ship to port abruptly, and that got a couple of "ooohs" from Doctor Etter, which made the rest of the groomsmen grin and even chuckle.

A minute later, the *Sword* landed in front of the enormous lodge, which was built with tossprho tree logs that were ten feet across.

The first member of the hunting party to disembark was Doctor Etter from the Barony Hospital Ship. Tanner thought he looked like he was in a bit of a rush to be back on solid ground. Bram was next and he smiled at the lodge staff lined up to greet them.

Major Alver Stal and Admiral McQueen were next and were still deep in conversation. They'd shared a row of seats and had talked about nothing but the ship off Ghayth. Thus far, they had not been able to come up with anything as an actionable plan.

Ahanu, the Ikarian from Throth, was all smiles. He was going hunting. He was as careful as he could be with his bow and arrows in their impenetrable case. No harm could come to them, but he babied the case nonetheless, as perhaps, Tanner thought, any real hunting race might.

The last three out of the *Sword* were Admiral Higgins, Prime Minister Lazaro, and Captain Craig Templeton of the *RN Marwick*. Three dear friends, Tanner knew, and he also knew they'd never hunted before either.

Rows of staff were spread out in front of the large

staircase that led up to the lodge. Bellmen and stewards, cooks and pantry girls, front desk staff, concierges, and even security officers stood waiting. Standing in front of the staff was Hunting Guide Master Koenig in his traditional hunter's garb of browns and greens. He was dressed as he always was in the forest shades of Anulet. Tanner noted that the holster on Koenig's side held a large revolver. The revolver was blue steel and had white grips. Small ammo leather boxes attached both in front and behind the holster.

A man like that—and then Tanner remembered guide master's body was probably one percent body fat—armed like that would be a force that could not be stopped.

Similarly dressed huntsmen surrounded the guide master, and they all bowed from the waist fully, held it for about fifteen seconds, and then straightened up at the same time.

Koenig took one step forward. A smile was plastered on his thin face, and his black brows arched over his gray eyes. With vigor and yet solemnness at the same time, he said, "Duke d'Avigdor—welcome to the Ducal Lodge on Anulet. We, your staff, wish you a hundred years and trophies for every wall you own, Duke!"

That got a cheer from the staff behind him, and he grinned even more.

"Your Grace, we have arranged for a nice lunch for you and your guests. Followed by an afternoon in the lodge armory first, followed by some weapons orientation and target practice, Duke. We'll go out on the hunt tomorrow after a light continental breakfast—and come in midafternoon or so with our trophies, and the grand hunting banquet is tomorrow evening for one and all," he finished off.

Tanner grinned at him. "If only, Guide Master, if only ..." and that got his guests all smiling too.

"It is too bad that Admiral Childs couldn't make it, Your Grace—I've hunted with him before, and he's a crack shot!" Koenig said.

"More for us," Bram quipped.

Everyone laughed as the guide master led them up the wide stairs into the lobby of the lodge. Massive logs, stacked on top of each other, formed the outer walls with smaller timbers used for interior walls and sections too. Behind the group, the staff hustled to accommodate the incoming guests. At the head of the group were nine concierges, who came to each guest and introduced themselves. There was one concierge for each guest, and the guests were led to their own particular rooms. Bellmen got the bags sorted in minutes and delivered each bag as quickly as possible.

However, Doctor Etter wouldn't let the staff

carry his black medical bag nor would Ahanu let anyone even get close to his case that carried his bow. Within an hour, they were all settled, and each made their way down the wide interior double staircase to the dining room off to one side of the lobby. Rows of floor-to-ceiling windows filled the room, and the view of the mountain range just a couple of miles away was stunning. Sunlight, red sunlight, shone down on the raw rock and made the darker heavily shadowed areas a rusty color. The deeper shadowed, reddish-brown-colored areas made it hard to see what might be a few feet ahead. *But we won't be way up there,* Tanner thought to himself as he entered the dining room and made his way to the large round table.

"No other guests?" he inquired nicely to the steward who immediately brought him a chilled glass and a pitcher of water.

"No, Your Grace, not these couple of days," he answered politely and went on to serve others too.

Lunch went fine and Tanner did enjoy the duck. At least he thought it was duck. It was a bird of some kind, all dark meat, with a sauce on the side that tasted both sweet and yet savory too, and he dipped each forkful in the sauce.

After lunch, the guide master, who had eaten at his right hand, stood to talk to the group. "With a hunting party of ten of us, we will split into two groups of five each. The duke, myself, Bram, Doctor Etter, and Captain Templeton in one group. And my second here," he said as he pointed at the man seated at the table but on the other side, "Hunting Guide Enola, will take out Major Stal, Admiral McQueen, Admiral Higgins, and Ahanu our Ikarian rep on the Confederacy Council. Will that work for everyone?" he inquired.

Already there were catcalls, and Alver made a bet on behalf of his team that the team who brought home the fewest trophies had to do the dishes after the big banquet tomorrow evening. Tanner's friends were all alpha males, and more of them began boasting. Additional side bets were made between the men as well.

Good to hear and see, Tanner thought, and as he looked around and smiled, Doctor Etter caught his eye and winked at him. *Good that perhaps the doctor sees the same as I do—but I won't mention anything today ...*

They laughed over the end of their lunch, and in a half hour, they were down in the bowels of the lodge in the secure armory to choose their arms for the hunt.

Tanner knew exactly what he wanted, and a Merkel appeared in front of him from one of the armory staff. He hoisted it up to his shoulder, worked the action a couple of times, and checked the balance and feel.

"This is good for me," he said and placed it down in front of him on the waist-high counter.

With the exception of Doctor Etter and Ahanu, everyone followed Tanner's lead and chose the Merkel. Doctor Etter was convinced to use a lighter carbine, a Remington, which shot a heavy steel-jacketed round and carried fifty rounds in the magazine. Ahanu, as Tanner knew he would, chose to use his bow.

The armory staff presented Ahanu with a variety of choices, but no amount of conversation or discussion would get him to change his mind. Armory staff had even asked for assistance from Koenig who had wandered over to inquire if there was an issue.

"No issue at all," Ahanu replied. "Just these persons think that my choice of weapon might be—what did one say—ancient, I think was used. Trust me, Guide Master, this is a weapon that I am well versed in using. If one of these Oveds comes across us even three hundred yards away, he's mine," the Ikarian said plainly.

That got a raised black eyebrow from Koenig, but he said not a word and motioned the armory staffer to walk away.

Twenty minutes later, they were all back up at ground level. Everyone went outside behind the lodge. Off to one side of the lodge was a low area that had berms all around it. Hunt staff there went through basic weapon orientation; safe weapons use; loading and unloading; jamming issues; how to clear the weapon; and how to set the safety and take it off.

Every single hunter went through that training, and all had paid enough attention to get a good to go from Guide Master Koenig.

Ahanu had stood and watched all of this, and he went over to speak to one of the staff for a moment when the training seemed to be over. The staffer took a target complete with a stand and jumped into a cart. He drove out to the farthest berm. He got out, set up the easel with the stand on it holding the target, and then drove all the way back. "Speedo says it's only two hundred and thirty-yards," he said.

Ahanu nodded as he lifted his weapon case onto the table in front of him. Opening the case, he took out his bow, which was constructed of black wood with what looked like gold inserts at the tips. It was a simple recurve bow, and Tanner remembered the Ikarians he'd met on the *Keshowse*, their sleeper ship, had used them well. *Never seen Ahanu use a bow so this outta be good*, Tanner thought.

The Ikarian stepped through the bow, bending one end, the tip, beneath his insole arch to hold the bow firmly. At the same time, he leaned on the bow more and more, as he slid the cord up and up until it locked into place in the bow nock, where it was meant to be. He reached into the case again and took out three arrows with his right hand. He stepped away from the table off to the side and then half-turned.

He had everyone's attention and Tanner hoped that the distance to the target wasn't too great, the winds weren't too strong, and that the target remained rock solid.

Two hundred and thirty yards—farther Tanner knew than he could shoot with any degree of accuracy. The Ikarian took a solid breath. And again. And then he took one more deep breath as he shifted into a square stance with his left foot forward and his right leg behind him.

His right hand, still carrying the three arrows at once, dove forward past the cord about halfway to the grip, and the right hand spun one arrow only to tuck it between his left thumb and the grip, while it pulled back and the arrow's nock slid into the cord at the same time. Ahanu pulled back strongly in one even pull. Both his eyes were open as he looked at the small target so far away and let the arrow loose. He repeated the same load, draw, and release action two more times. All three arrows were sent in less than a second and a half. Eyebrows rose at the speed that all arrows were released, and everyone looked out at the target, but it was too far away to see the results.

Ahanu lifted his left foot, nodded to a member of the hunting staff, and asked that he simply go and get the target and return it. The staff member commented that he'd be sure to not disturb anything on the target, and he drove the cart away in moments.

He returned quickly with the target still on the easel, standing up in the back of the cart. Everyone crowded around and there were several exclamations of "Oh my God" and even "You gotta be kidding me" from someone.

Tanner didn't bother to go look but stood staring at Ahanu. "You okay with that shoot," he asked.

Ahanu shrugged. "First one is off slightly, but other two are fine," he said as he stepped back into the recurve bow to take the cord. He placed the bow carefully in the case and locked his weapon up once more. For him, there was no issue with what had just happened.

Bram waved Tanner over, and since the suspense was killing him, he ambled the twenty feet to look at the target. Two arrows were so close to the dead center of the rings that they were touching each other. The one arrow that was a whole inch off center was the first one Ahanu had said. Probably finding wind and range and all the things that an archer might have to know to hit a target. "Or kill an Oved, even ..." Tanner said to himself, and he nodded to Guide Master Koenig, whose black brows were still arched up in surprise.

"The hunt was tomorrow ... and that should be promising ..." Tanner said to himself as they all took their weapons and went back into the lodge to put them away until then.

Dinner came and went. They'd all laughed a lot at the stories Admiral McQueen had told of earlier days as a captain and how Admiral Higgins had tried to outdo his stories with ones of his own.

Alver grinned, tossed back beer after beer, laughing with the rest of them, and added some stories of his own about life as a marine. Captain Templeton joshed back at Alver about how marines on his ship couldn't hold their liquor, and that got a round of shots all around.

They laughed a lot, Tanner saw as he too told a story or two. One story was about a night on Conclusion that he barely remembered and how he'd stolen a robo-cab from right under the Lady St. August's nose—and he got a bigger laugh when he reminded them that she never let him forget it either.

Bram, however, was pretty quiet he noticed. The drinks and sharing of stories were slowing down, and a couple of the hunting party had already retired.

Tanner went over to sit beside his best friend. "You okay, there, Bram?" he said quietly as Alver was imitating a dance he said he'd seen over on Lurdar called the LuLuLurch, and that was getting roars from the smaller group gathered down at the far end of the table.

Bram nodded but he said, "Can I just touch your arm—I've news and I want you to see it as plainly as possible?"

Tanner nodded and he stuck out his arm. Bram slid a hand over his forearm and squeezed. Tanner's mind was slowly gripped by a tendril from Bram's mind, and he kept calm.

From what he could see, he realized it was from days ago, and as he watched, he saw Bram resign from the Issian faith and the Master Adept acknowledging same. He also saw Bram had stated the truth to the head of his faith. He meant what he said about not using his mind reading talent to enrich himself but to help others.

As that was the last thing that Bram sent to him, Tanner smiled at his friend. He turned slightly to face Bram. "I am surprised at your choice—not that you felt like you needed to leave the faith, but that it happened now?"

Bram nodded. "It was because I felt that it would

be more honest to you to leave the Issian faith. As you know, we swear allegiance within that faith to the Master Adept—and I felt that anything that I learned and knew no longer should be passed along to the Master whenever she asked for updates. So I left. But that just means that I take off the ringed planet badge. I am no longer an Adept officer in the Duchy Navy ... so ..." he said.

"No matter, still my best lieutenant commander —don't even worry about it," Tanner said. Though Bram had given up—resigned actually from—the Issian faith, his mind was still a working organ and he was loyal to Tanner.

Bram half-turned to face the duke. "But there is one more thing too ... it's Gia," he said stoically.

Tanner stopped cold. "Gia? What about her?" he asked, his blood pressure rising as he went red in the face.

"Your Grace, you should know that I intend to woo and then wed your sister," Bram said, his voice now fervent.

Tanner froze. He sputtered for a moment or two. His face emptied of blood, as he got his psyche moving backward toward equilibrium.

He noted that his left hand was tapping a one-two, one-two pattern over and over on his knee, which was the PTSD aid he'd been taught by the doctor. He breathed slowly.

Bram was in love with Gia—having never been alone with her or seeing her anywhere besides at Tanner's wedding and in court at her trial. That was a shock.

Wonder what will happen with this whole schmozzle? he thought as he looked over at Bram. "Bram ... then that might mean we'd be brothers-in-law, would it not?" he asked, a grin appearing on his face.

Bram looked so relieved that his face was aglow, and then he gripped Tanner by the shoulders and hugged him.

Big hug, Tanner thought, *Big hug that lasts and lasts ...*

He hugged his friend back, and they called for two more drinks—a scotch for Bram and a juice shooter for Tanner.

Brothers-in-law ... that has a nice, nice sound to it ...

Captain McDonald sat in the station cafeteria, nursing his smoothie. It had taken a few months for the station to be barged into its low orbit around Ghayth from the shipyards in Neres. He'd been lax these past few months and had skipped the gym completely. Now, he went every day before his shift on the bridge, and he tore the hell out of the rowing machine and the free weights.

He had been more than a little surprised with the changes that came from three months of inactivity. He could no longer do a standing military press of two hundred and forty pounds in countdown repetitions from five to one. He had been okay for the first set of repetitions, but then the second was painful, and he couldn't even get to the three-two-one set at all. His triceps burned, and his poorly repaired rotator cuff on his left arm screamed at him. And once again, he said the hell with the gym and working out.

Instead of being in the gym, he sat at a table in the cafeteria with a smoothie. *At least I chose a healthy smoothie,* he thought, but he didn't know for sure since he had stopped the juice bar attendant from rattling off the list of ingredients and health benefits. He slowly consumed his smoothie. *By the end of the week, I should be okay with the reps and sets for my standing military press.*

At least he hoped so, and he turned to look out the big viewport window on the exterior bulkhead that showed, as it had now for nineteen days, the alien ship.

Still poised where it had appeared.

Still totally quiet and sealed off.

Still an unknown.

He knew that the last shuttle to go over there had also met the force field and had been unable to penetrate same, of course. But whether or not the aliens could even see them and acknowledge them was the real question.

He shook his head. It was above his pay grade to worry about anything else but the space station, the *Wilson*, and himself.

His job was to run and manage same.

Of course, he'd not ever considered this kind of an alien occurrence with the resulting parade of RIM Confederacy bigwigs dropping by for a look-see. Not at all.

The chairman of the RIM Confederacy Council had arrived and taken a shuttle. While he had heard the repeated request from Chairman Gramsci to acknowledge that the RIM Confederacy wanted to talk, the aliens were incommunicado.

Not a peep. Nor was there any response for the Baroness who'd done almost the same thing, nor for Admiral McQueen, the head of the RIM Navy, nor the new Duke d'Avigdor, nor the Narrisol of Tillion, nor the Gerent Northos of KappaD. Not a single bigwig could get a thing out of the aliens.

However, the Baroness had issued a martial law edict on Ghayth, and all nonessential Barony staff was being sent off planet, back to Neres, he'd heard. There was still a large contingent up in the arctic and a smaller group exploring the southern hemisphere too.

He also knew there had been a large influx—a full division—of Barony marines. They had arrived and had moved down to the planet mostly. Almost a company and a half were, however, being billeted here on the station, and that resulted in traffic increases at the cafeterias at meal times. But, as he knew, that was a good thing. Having marines all over did make for a more settled type of feeling for the station staff, and he'd been told that by many here too.

He slurped more of his smoothie, noting that once in a while, pieces of something went by his tongue, and he refused to try to think about what it might have been. Instead, he just shook his head and thought, *Healthy … it's healthy …* and he grinned to no one in particular.

His thoughts drifted back to the recent meeting arranged by the Baroness. Even though he felt it was above his pay grade, McDonald had been invited to attend. Chairman Gramsci and the other important higher-ups had discussed what to do about the alien ship.

Bomb them, set a shot over their bows, and completely enclose them with mines were some options presented. All adversarial options had been dismissed.

The chairman had put it best, he thought, *when he had said, "We are going to wait for what they want to happen and react. We are not going to be proactive at all."*

"At least for starters," the station captain said to himself as he slurped the tail endings of the smoothie. He stood and tossed the empty cup into the recycling bin at the doorway, on his way back to his quarters.

Shower, put on my uniform, and go to the bridge are what lay in front of me now.

He wished he knew what was coming from the mile-long alien ship off the station's bow. He had a feeling it would be unlike anything they had ever encountered before.

#####

As the Master Adept stepped into the normally hidden and sealed room off her private study and quarters in the tower, she shuddered for a second. "Someone must have just walked on my grave," she said to herself and then laughed out loud. "That superstition is as old as the last few millennia," she said to herself, and she went in to sit at the small table inside the secret room.

She knew that she had to go into that room.

How she knew, she did not know, but she knew it was time.

Like all citizens of the RIM Confederacy, she

129

knew there was a ship moored off Ghayth, and while others thought of it as an alien ship, she knew it was the Praix.

When they had "winked into being" those seventy lights away from Eons, she had felt them arrive and had known they had a problem. They were fleeing from an enemy they could not defeat. An enemy who, for whatever reason, was moving from system to system, and after some kind of a hidden audit of the world within that system, the enemy usually set the world's sun to explode in a nova via a bomb that made the star explode.

These invaders in SagD were slowly working on turning out the lights all across that galaxy.

The Praix were unable to stop them. Each time they went in for an attack, the invader ships were invulnerable, and they destroyed the Praix ships with some kind of a weapon that exploded the ships entirely.

The Master Adept had received that information about twenty days ago; it was knowledge that was sent to the Issian race from their masters, the Praix, via a mind send message.

Since then, the Praix had been silent, but she knew, or at least she thought she knew, what it was they were awaiting.

She had convened a mind group meeting immediately. The Issian inner circle—the twelve most talented Issians—had met to discuss this new emergency and what they could do.

The large tome had been passed down to her from the previous Master Adept and was filled with more than twenty thousand years of the secrets of her race and the Praix all spelled out. As she pulled the book onto her lap, she remembered the yelling at that first mind group meeting of the Issian inner circle. Some were all for out and out war with the Praix, beside and with the RIM Confederacy realms. Others preached to wait, to see what would happen, and to pick a side when the winner could be foreseen to hedge their bets. One had said to just leave—get in ships and go inwards perhaps all the way through the Milky Way Galaxy to the RIM on the other side.

Nothing had been decided.

As the Master Adept, she had information via the book on her lap that the rest did not have, but she had not shared any of the information with the others.

Every day now, for more than three weeks almost, the inner circle had met, and the arguments had gone one way and then the other; some days, the arguments had gone in a totally new direction.

One thing that could not be missed by all was that the Praix were doing nothing but sitting off Ghayth. Alone. Solitary. And waiting.

She had thought her own position through many times and had no one else to go to for counsel. But yesterday, she had finally known that she could not keep silent any longer.

She was concerned with the future of her Issian race, and that meant she had to tell all ... and the only way for that to happen was to open up her mind to the inner circle—in its entirety.

The link yesterday was strong but made so because she had demanded they all attend to her here, on Eons, in the tower in the walled city. That got some squawks, but she had been insistent, and as she was the Master Adept, they had to obey. Most had arrived quickly with the new Barony Drive, and only one had been a bit late coming in from Faraway via a trader vessel.

They had sat, and she had spoken first.

She had tried to tell them about the need for secrecy about what she was going to divulge to them.

She had tried to let them know that she was, as far as she knew, the first Master Adept who had allowed others to know about the Praix and their book and their secrets.

She had played for them the video that showed the spokesperson for the Praix, who had shown the viewer their home world and cities.

She had let them know that the Praix were a

different race, body-wise, and there had been a couple of gasps when the Praix had shown himself at the start of that video. The Praix was avian with a fifteen-foot-wide wingspan, a small orange beak on a balding head, and full-feathered growth on the body and wings.

"Sort of a vulture but huge," she said to herself, but she did not share that analogy with the others.

She had let the video play through to the end, and some had said the Praix home world in SagD was beautiful, and they were right.

She had then had them all link hands, and she had opened up her mind completely to let them see —as only a skin-to-skin contact between Issians can —what she knew that they did not.

In any such link of twelve minds, there was always an ebb and flow, and in this case, the feeling she got was one of draining her, her psyche, her own consciousness, as the inner circle learned what secrets the book held.

There were many things therein that now, twenty thousand years later, she was ashamed of, shuddered to even consider, and could not even countenance. The death of races and planets, and yes, the Issian way of helping the Praix subdue planet after planet of newly conquered aliens. She had read the book completely over the past year since she'd inherited the Master Adept role, and she opened up for everything to be freely seen by the other minds now linked to her mind.

In less than a minute, the complete contents of the Praix book had been shared, and she dropped the hands of the inner circle members on either side of her, signifying that the deepest part of their mind meld was over.

They sat. Not a single word was said until she spoke after almost ten minutes of silence.

"So you see the issue we now face. This Praix ship with less than a hundred souls on board is here. This is a new galaxy to them. Their technology is superior to all that we have, and from what we know, for any other races here as well.

"The fact that they are evading a superior race back in their own galaxy does not matter to us or to them. They are here to assume the top of the food chain position they know, or think they know, is rightfully theirs," she said.

"And, they want us to acknowledge our presence and to once again swear allegiance to them as our masters—and to help them to conquer this galaxy beginning, I believe, with the RIM Confederacy."

She stopped then, and there had been no talk at all.She sighed. It was too much most likely to digest all at once. It had taken her a full year to read the book and to fathom out the details that were unwritten about the relationship between the Praix and the Issians.

They were our masters, and we were their slave keepers, she thought as she shivered a second or two. *And do we want to re-enact our roles as such, at the top of the food chain, but as slave masters for the Praix?*

Today, she had called them all back to get the communal decision made, and the last ones had just left.

The message from them all—the eleven other members of the inner circle—had weighed the import of what Issians had been and were now. And what they might become.

There had been no equivocation or ambiguity from all of the inner circle minds.

No. The Issians would not allow themselves to be subjugated by the Praix once again and return to the role of helping them conquer a new galaxy.

Instead, they would help the RIM Confederacy to fight and defeat the Praix and rid the Milky Way of this foe.

She had nodded and she agreed.

But that final point that they would help fight the Praix was the one thing she knew would be impossible at this point. With drastically superior technology, anyone could defeat those with lesser weapons and defenses too.

The Praix were the most advanced, and the RIM would need to find a way to take the fight to them

... and win.

She sighed, as she once again opened the big tome on her knees and began to read the book again. Maybe t she'd missed something; maybe if she read "between the lines," something would pop out.

There had to be a way to defeat the Praix. *With more than three hundred million inhabitants on Eons, I have more than some skin in this game ...*

Hunting Guide Master Koenig smiled at them as he dropped his rifle on his shoulder and pointed out to the left of where the two hunting parties stood. The helicopter ride had taken only a half hour, and they had been deposited on a meadow partway up a large set of ridges to their left while below them were the ravines and drop-offs that were wooded almost completely. Ahead of them, the meadow slanted up slightly to an area where there were copses of trees and thick cover, and when Tanner turned his head to the rear, he saw the same behind him.

"What we're going to do is to split up here. This meadow—I've sent the coordinates to each team member's PDA in case you get lost—is home base. I'll take the duke, Bram, the doc, and Captain Templeton ahead slowly working our way up the slopes. The other team of the major, Admirals McQueen and Higgins, and Ahanu will go with Hunting Guide Enola toward the rear, working their way down the slopes. We intend to cover almost ten miles today—five out and then back. And no, we can't get the copter in any closer to pick up any lazybones," he said with a smile.

That got some grins, and Bram elbowed the doctor in the ribs, and that too got a laugh.

Once everyone settled down, Koenig finished with his instructions. "So, let's get some things straight. We're going to move quietly—we're going to not talk or laugh. We will spread out and we walk with a degree of caution. An Oved is big—at least ten feet at the shoulder and weighing half a ton—and those racks of horns are not carried by them to put up on our hunting lodge walls. They use them to attack—something you must always have in mind. Rifles on safety, please, don't take it off 'til I okay your shot," he finished off, and moments later, the two teams were walking away from the home base meadow toward their quarry.

Tanner had read the short summary that Koenig had sent to each of them sometime last night, and at breakfast just an hour or so ago, the information had been discussed.

The doctor had said he had no idea why they didn't just round up some of these Oveds and then

137

they could shoot whichever ones they liked. That got some raised eyebrows and a rant about what was sporting when it came to hunting and what was plain butchery from Alver. He capitulated quickly on his statement, but that got them talking about hunting in general, and then they zoomed off on Oveds and why they were such a trophy. Horns, Admiral Higgins said, were the big draw, and they all nodded at that.

As the team began to walk toward their assigned hunting grounds, Admiral McQueen sidled up to Tanner for a quiet word.

"Duke, I have a request—well, in fact it's an order, but as a new Royal, you might not be familiar with the full RIM Confederacy Constitution, Your Grace," he said a bit apologetically.

"It means that as the head of the RIM Confederacy Navy, I have the right to assign—in times of troubles—roles to anyone I see fit. And you're up, son!" he said with a grin.

Tanner looked at his mentor and smiled. "Whatever it is—I'm always sure that coming from you, Admiral, it'll be a doozy!"

The admiral grinned at him and went on. "The RIM Navy is forming a task force to deal with these aliens ... the intruders off Ghayth. I have spoken to each of the other members of the executive committee, and they are all in agreement with my decision.

"You have been appointed as the head of the task force, but you will have the full support of the RIM Confederacy and, yes, each of the realms in the committee too. The Baroness, who owns the Ghayth planet, is also behind you. You are her 'golden boy,' my lad, for sure," the admiral said with a tone of wonder in his voice.

Tanner nodded. Sure, being the new leader of the Task Force was mostly an honorary position — unless the task force was charged with a mandate to rid the RIM of the alien intruders. That might pose a problem. While his mind went off on that tangent, he also suddenly realized that being the leader meant other things as well. One of which made him smile as he realized he now had the right to ask other navies on the RIM for loans of equipment and better navy personnel.

Now, that might work out well, he thought as he followed the doctor now, and the meadow got deeper in depth as the grasses were more overgrown.

As Tanner walked, he noted they followed Koenig and walked in a straight line, and they did so for almost a mile, as the meadow disappeared. At that point, they entered a lightly wooded treed slope. As they entered the trees, Koenig stopped and waited while everyone caught up with him.

In a low undertone, he said, "Here's where we'll spread out ... Duke, you go in about, say, one hundred yards, and then turn to your right and try to follow the edge of the trees—then the doctor, then Bram, and lastly the captain. I'll stay here on the edge of the woods and the meadow as it meanders along. Use me to mark your place and speed, but do NOT go quickly. Walk normally—Oveds have great hearing, and it's important that you sound like another Oved to a bull that might be resting, bedded in the woods. I've got a cow call on your PDA—turn it on, and it will make that call to alleviate any strangeness a bull might be feeling as you walk toward them. It will play when it needs to —and yes, we do know from past hunting trips that bulls often take some siesta time here in this big tree stand."

"It made sense," Tanner said to himself as he nodded and took the lead turning to his left and slowly and quietly walked deeper into the woods. Unlike his last trip to Anulet when he and the late duke had been after Jaels, those huge bear-like creatures, these woods were less thick. and he could see ahead at least fifty or so yards before the trunks closed off his sight. He dodged around some of the lighter smaller trunks—aspens, he thought, as the bark was a light green in color. Eventually his PDA throbbed on his wrist. He had gone far enough, and he then turned to his right to move ahead through the copse.

To his right, he could see the doctor and then Bram was next, but he couldn't see who else was there.

He walked slowly. He was careful to not make a sound—and the first cow call that seeped out of his PDA made him jump. If that's what a female Oved sounded like, he was sure they led a solitary life. He shook his head and pushed through a clump of some kind of deep overgrowth, down a dip, and up the other side. *Hunting. I'm hunting and it's fun.* He had to tell himself that already more than once and that made him smile. This trip was for his groomsmen to help put some closure on the murders at his wedding more than a year ago. And it appeared, at least so far, to be working okay.

He pushed a group of branches off some kind of a fir tree and stepped around a bigger one ahead as he noted that here, deeper in the woods, the trees were getting closer together.

His PDA throbbed, and he looked down at it. It had one word on it: STOP.

So he stopped. And he waited. Well to his right, he knew his hunting group was spread out, and he could now only see the doctor who was also stopped. He moved a little to get a better line of sight around some particularly thick cover, and yes, he could see Bram, but he was still walking.

He thought that perhaps Koenig was doing some kind of a wheeling maneuver—anchor him and the doctor at one spot, and then have the others walk to drive any bulls toward him.

He grinned. Hunting was okay, and he hoisted the Merkel to now sit on his shoulder at rest, From behind a tight group of trees about thirty yards to his right, a bull Oved was hoisting itself up and out of the deep cover.

He grinned again. The bull was walking stiff-legged at first, working out any kinks perhaps, and then the stupid cow call went off on his PDA.

The bull stopped short, and up went his head to sniff and look toward Tanner. The Oved was massive, at least the proverbial ten feet at the shoulder, and the huge rack of horns was shiny, bright, and full of tines.

He slowly, very slowly, moved the rifle a bit, trying to find the safety with his right thumb as the rifle sat upside down on his right shoulder.

"Where ... where was that damn—got it," he said to himself as his finger carefully and quietly slid the safety off.

He knew he was frozen in this pose until the Oved decided what to do, and as he pondered that, there was a loud bang of a shot, and the Oved

142

sprung to its left and dove out of Tanner's sight.

"What the hell," he said to himself as he leapt ahead and tried to follow the huge animal as he heard the doctor yelling, "I got him ... I got him."

After Tanner dodged around a smaller group of saplings, he could see the Oved. It was charging the doctor who was jumping up and down looking around—and not at the Oved that bore down at him.

"Doc—find cover," he screamed as he pointed the gun at the Oved as it closed on the doctor.

The doctor was surprised by first the Oved that he now saw charging at him—then at what Tanner had shouted from twenty or so yards away. Somehow, he dove to the ground and rolled to try to dodge the quickly closing Oved.

Tanner had one shot as he stopped and waited a whole two seconds as the Oved moved out from behind the trees and toward the doctor's position. He squeezed off a single round at the area behind the Oved's front left leg into his chest, and yet the Oved didn't even slow down.

The Oved also dropped its head to gore the doctor who was lying on the ground, and it must have gotten lucky as the doctor cried out in pain. The Oved raised its head, its feet now scrabbling to get away, and it charged back the way the hunting team had come, crashing through the undergrowth and right through smaller saplings.

Tanner had reached the doctor's side, and as he did, he pushed the emergency button on his PDA and was happy to hear all of his team come crashing through the woods toward them.

He turned the doctor over and noted the man's face was frozen in pain. He turned the doctor to one side and saw blood seeping out where the Oved had gored the doctor. The horn had first hit the light hunting parka and then entered the doctor as the Oved bore down on the doctor. The Oved's horn had left a piercing hole. That was where some of the blood was coming, but as the Oved had lifted its head after that piercing, the horn had then ripped open a long furrow of skin, and that was the main source of blood loss. The Oved's horn had torn the doctor open from just below the shoulder blade down almost to the waist.

"Let me see," Koenig said as he pulled off his pack and whipped out a small first aid field kit. He used a knife to open up the doctor's parka, noted the wound, and nodded. "Not lethal. But the doc won't be dancing a jig for a while," he said as he quickly ripped open a package of white powder and poured it all over the wounds. He reached into the field kit, took out a pain pen, and jammed it into the doctor's upper arm—twice, Tanner noted—and in moments, the doctor was no longer yelling in pain.

"I can't see the wound ..." Doctor Etter said.

"Psychiatrists don't need to see wounds," Koenig said nicely as he began to bandage up the wounds. Long butterfly tapes went on the furrows before and after the gore piercing. For it, he packed the hole with some antiseptic gauze and then slapped a round bandage on same.

As the rest of the team stood around, Koenig rose.

"I've called the copter back, and we'll get out of here double-quick. But a hunting post-mortem is in order. Doc—you were way out of line to shoot the Oved ... it was too close, it was startled, and it was more than able to defend itself. Next time, wait. See which way the wind is blowing. It could obviously smell you and the cow call was not a factor. It knew it was in trouble, and if you'd stood and waited, it would have gone on away from you. But that shot —you must have hit it—got it's dander up, and you paid for that. Thank god we were hunting Oveds and not Jaels," he said as he flung a sideways glance at Tanner.

Right. Good advice, Tanner thought, and he picked up the doctor's rifle. Craig helped the doctor by offering up a shoulder, and they all prepared to leave the wooded area. Koenig did not head back toward the meadow but led them through the wooded area.

Tanner tapped Koenig on the shoulder. "It would be easier walking if we headed back to the meadow, especially with an injured man. Any reason why we are still in the woods?"

Koenig replied, "Because, Duke, we have an injured animal ahead of us—so we need to fix that before we leave the woods."

They continued walking with Koenig at the front, following a path the Oved had obviously taken—judging by the small groups of trampled weeds and the branches ripped out of trees overhead. Koenig paused to look at some of those lower markings, and in one case, everyone saw some drops of blood.

As they came up a small rise, Koenig held up a hand. "Let's take a moment, shall we? The Oved is ahead."

Tanner went right up to stand beside the guide master, and down below them in a swale of thick weeds was the Oved, lying on its side, breathing hoarsely. Koenig held out a hand to prevent Tanner from doing anything, and moments later the Oved shook all over, and its breathing stopped.

Koenig moved the safety on his own rifle to off and went around the swale to stand on the other side. He gently walked down a step or two and pushed the Oved's massive rack of horns with a foot, keeping the rifle aimed directly at the beast.

"Dead—he's dead, right?" the doctor croaked.

Koenig nodded. "Took a shot to the lungs—they filled with blood—and yup, he just died. Good shot, Duke," he said.

Tanner wasn't sure it had been his shot, and he had to say so. "But Guide Master—the doctor shot the animal first—maybe it is his kill," he said.

"Yes, he did, but that bullet hit the Oved here," he said as he pushed on the rack of horns, and they could all see that the rack looked huge and perfect —except for one point. "See this point? A G5, I'd say, that is so newly broken off that I make the call that this is what the doctor shot.

"Imagine what it might be like to be startled out of a sleep, rise, and then get a big point shot off your rack. Would make the whole Oved head ring like a bell—no wonder he turned to attack the doc— umm, that yelling didn't help much either."

The doctor nodded. "It definitely is the duke's kill," he said which ended the matter.

As the whole team walked around to look at the Oved, Koenig was busy making a note of the exact location of the kill on his hunting PDA so the lodge staff could retrieve same later. They did also take a moment, over Tanner's protests, to take some pictures. Tanner's friends would hear not a word as an excuse, and they had Tanner drop down to his knees to kneel beside the Oved for some of the pictures.

As they walked back, Koenig said, "Will make a wonderful trophy, Duke—with that missing point, the story can be told that will make folks laugh right out loud," he said, his smile broad.

Tanner nodded as they left the huge wood stand and headed toward the helicopter that awaited them. *Back to the lodge and then the dinner and then back to Neen*, Tanner thought, *but one thing is hopefully done—that my friends now have a new experience to think on, whenever any of them looked back ... the wedding now hidden behind the Oved hunt on Anulet ...*

CHAPTER FIVE

The drone ship came in from sub-space, and as usual, the Ghayth station had no clue a ship was arriving. Long-range sensors were unable to track inbound ships because of the speed of the new Barony Drive; therefore, ships arrived before the long-range scanners even sounded a gong.

Not that this was a ship really; it was a drone ship, about two hundred feet long, with the usual Ansible arrays and the Impulse drive that any ship used at sub-light speeds. The drone ship was now turning to its starboard side, lining up to face the Praix ship more than thirty times bigger. That bothered the helmsman on the *Wilson*, and he hit the alarm button right away.

The alien ship sent out its usual ultra-bright teal ray, and it touched the drone ship for a second or two. Nobody had any idea yet what that ray did; all anyone knew was that any ship close enough to the alien ship was bathed in that teal ray.

Klaxons sounded and Captain McDonald, who had been just outside the bridge door talking to someone from engineering, strode in to take the captain's chair. "Klaxons off, please, Helmsman," he said, and he stared at what lay in front of the space station.

Fixed in space in low orbit, the *Wilson* was almost ten miles off the alien ship that hung at the same orbital altitude.

Beside the station lay three Barony ships—the frigate the *Coventry*, and two cruisers, the *Whitney* and the *Newton*. They were poised to help protect the space station via their own weaponry should it be needed.

But this new drone ship lay off to one side, and as McDonald watched, it was now closing on the huge alien craft.

"Ansible, call that drone—if there's anyone on board—and get them to back off; tell them we've got the situation in hand," he barked, and his Ansible officer was soon using her throat mic, but it looked like it was to no avail as the drone continued to close.

"Ansible, hail the navy ships, I want that drone stopped before it causes an incident. ASAP,

Lieutenant," he said, his voice rising.

As the frigate moved out toward the drone ship and the *Whitney* followed, McDonald had a sick feeling about it.

"Sir, no one aboard that drone—RIM ID puts it as a Novertag drone, Sir—but I can't get through to them either. Some kind of a thermal storm in their system, it appears, Sir," she said as she once again covered her face with the megaphone part of her throat mic and began to try to raise someone before something happened.

McDonald was on his feet before he knew it, and he barked again to his Ansible crewwoman. "Urgent EYES ONLY to Admiral McQueen, pipe through our full data to him—vid and analytics too. I want this recorded, and I want—"

The flash of a nuke as it met the force field around that alien ship was intense, and the filters slammed into place over the view-screen on the *Wilson*. The huge red and yellow intense beams of light as the tactical nuke went off were bright enough to make a man go blind for a few hours until the photonic entropy of that blast would wear off, and McDonald was grateful the filters had snapped up so quickly. Despite the filters, he had flashing spots all across his field of vision, but there was still work to do.

"Ansible, to the *Whitney*—code Station 9-DD6—

destroy that drone now," he said.

With no one aboard, he was risking only hardware, but that meant any further ordnance on the drone ship would also go off when the Whitney used her energy pulse cannon to bomb the drone ship out of existence.

But before that could even be sent, the force field around the alien ship suddenly glowed a deep, deep violet. From that field, a lobe reached out toward the drone still miles away, and it covered that distance in less than a second. It touched the drone ship—and the drone ship disappeared.

Nothing else happened. There were no further explosions of other ordnance nor was there any ship debris.

The drone ship had just disappeared—in its entirety.

The long lobe of that purple color slowly sank back inside the force field, which slowly faded from violet to being invisible as it usually was seen.

"Ansible, belay that order to the Whitney, have her return to her station," he said.

The bridge was quiet. He pondered what he'd just seen. "Science?" he said quietly.

Behind him at the science console, the station expert on all things about science shrugged. "Sir, I've no idea. What we just saw was an unprovoked attack on the alien vessel, which was handled by them on their own. My own gauges and analytics showed a 1.8 percent increase in the power levels of the force field they use to cover their ship as it reached out somehow to simply make the drone ship disappear. I've no idea on what kind of science that might be—past my ken is what I'm saying, Sir. But I did just see it with my own eyes ..." he finished, his voice a bit frustrated sounding to his captain.

McDonald nodded. "Sent to Admiral McQueen, yes?" he asked, and that got a response.

"Sir, sent but we are also advised that the admiral is on Anulet with a hunting party, Sir," back from his Ansible officer.

"Roger that," McDonald said, "and I want that RIM ID sent as well—why Novertag would have sent a drone to attack the aliens is beyond me—but notify the RIM Confederacy Council clerk of this as well—send her the data too—I'd guess that they're going to have to answer for that but not here and today," he said.

He shook his head. "Stay on that alien vessel. They were just attacked, and their force field held off that nuke, and they took out the offending ship on their own. Full, as usual, analytics and archive the lot too," he said.

As the *Coventry* and the *Whitney* were repositioning themselves to flank the space station, he watched the alien ship. Nothing. Not a single thing happened as a result of the attack. At least nothing he could see, nor for that matter that the *Wilson* could see with all its technology either.

"So, we sit once again," he said to himself.

#####

It was his first executive committee meeting. Tanner was ready for anything, but he knew today's meeting would not be a normal one. On his way up, he had followed the seven RIM Navy Provost guards who were escorting Captain Evgeny Pankov of the Novertag ship the *Drozir*, between them. As the *Sword* had set down on the Juno navy base landing port, he'd seen the *Drozir* just a few pads away, and he had watched as this man was escorted off their ship and taken directly to Navy Hall.

He almost smiled to himself and then remembered that a duke would never broadcast what he was thinking to those around him. That was a lesson Helena tried to drill into him, but he replied that it was easier to just look beautiful as a woman, and no man ever thought about anything more than that.

She had laughed at him just an evening ago, and that had made his whole day. The next day, the attack on the alien ship off Ghayth had happened and that was what today's emergency meeting was all about. All full executive committee members would be in attendance to determine the fate of the two Novertag military officers who had been identified as the responsible parties in the attack on the alien ship.

While Tanner had his doubts, he'd met Captain Pankov once before—almost ten years ago—when the Novertag realm had been bidding on taking over the Ikarians—and their sleeper ship. He'd been in communication back then with Premier Leonid Sigalov, who had pointed the finger to this captain. He'd met that captain too and was not impressed— the man's bare ambition seemed to overshadow everything else in the man's life—including his ability to be a starship captain too.

At the fifth floor, the Provost guards marched the Novertag Navy man down the hall, and he followed their lead. At the doorway to the committee meeting room, he saw there were already some members present, and he was greeted with a wave to come in from Admiral McQueen. He followed his lead to the empty seat to sit directly to the admiral's right at the round table, and he made his smiles and introductions to the rest at the table. To the left of the admiral sat the Master Adept—the new one, he meant—and then the Baroness who smiled at him as she was sipping a glass of something green. To her left was an empty seat with the Doge of Conclusion written on the name holder place card. The Doge of Conclusion must be running late today, Tanner thought. Next to the Doge's empty seat, the chairman of the RIM Confederacy Council, Chairman Gramsci, sat, and all six of his hands were busy with files, documents, and two tablets. Finally the last seat held the Caliph —Sharia Al Dotsa—who was on Tanner's right.

Seven members composed of the four largest realms, the official chairman, the vice chairperson, and the RIM Navy head admiral were to determine what would happen to the Novertag officers. The seven members were charged with the duty of meeting as often as might be required to work on items that would be of import to the whole Confederacy Council itself.

"Now, I have a seat on this committee," Tanner said to himself. "And now, we have an issue that needs our counsel and advice. For the good of the Confederacy."

He looked over at the far wall at the Novertag Navy captain, and for a moment, he felt this meeting would not only be his first but perhaps the most difficult he might ever face.

But enough about what might happen, he thought. From across the table, he saw the Master Adept dip her head, and he grinned at her. If she had caught that, then good—and the hell with trying to maintain a poker face. Surely here, in these circumstances, with peers, he could be himself.

The Master Adept dipped her head again as Chairman Gramsci tapped his forefinger on the table and opened the meeting.

"Let's get this show on the road," Chairman Gramsci said, and he looked over at the admiral. "And Admiral, please, we'd like to see the video first, if we could?"

The admiral nodded and made a couple of clicks on his tablet. They all turned to watch the big vid screen on the interior wall. Five minutes later, the vid ended, and the chairman spoke once again.

"As you saw, from somewhere, a drone ship appeared, took up an attack mode against the alien ship, and launched a tactical nuke against the alien ship. It went off—and nothing happened. The captain of the *Wilson*, the Ghayth space station, ordered a frigate and a cruiser to take the drone into custody, I assume, but the aliens instead somehow made the drone ship disappear. With what I'd call a quick answer to our attack—that purple lobe of color came off the alien ship's force field, I'd say. And then nothing. But we're not here today to work on the alien ship problem," he said.

He looked over at the Provost guards and motioned for them to bring the prisoner closer. He was pushed by a couple of the guards and stood off to one side of the table, his hands in restraints at his waist.

I know this man, Tanner thought, *and he was a poor captain—but that's not here nor there.*

Still in his captain's uniform, Pankov stared straight ahead at attention as good as he could muster while his hands were so immobile.

"What do you have to say, Captain," Chairman Gramsci asked politely.

The captain looked like he had an answer at the ready, and he met no eyes but spoke in a matter-of-fact tone.

"It came to our attention—Novertag's attention, that is—that the alien ship was holding off Ghayth with no communication. It was our opinion—which we acted on—that the only way we might get these aliens to respond was to knock on their front door. Hence, the nuke—which we knew, as did all RIM Confederacy citizens, that cannot pierce a force field. The assumption was correct, and we were as surprised as you were that the aliens chose to simply destroy the drone ship. Incidentally, this is why we sent in a drone ship—an unmanned craft that risked no lives," he said, his voice still plain with no emotion showing.

The chairman tapped on the tabletop, but he was just marking time, Tanner thought. The admiral

158

had a look on his face that said "bullshit." As he looked around the table, Tanner saw the same look, but a little more tempered, was also shown on the faces of the Doge, the Baroness, and the Caliph.

The only face that did not show any degree of astonishment belonged to the Master Adept, who leaned forward to speak. "Chairman, if I may ..." she began.

"Of course, Master Adept, do go on," said Gramsci who wanted to know what the only mind reader in the room might have seen.

She nodded and then looked down at the bare burnished wood of the table in front of her. She never brought anything to a meeting, Tanner would learn, and she had pushed the empty desk pad to one side, placing her bare arms on the warm wood of the table itself.

She looked around the table. She looked up and a bit to her left at the Novertag captain, and then she smiled. "What this young man has just said to us— is absolutely true. In his mind, I see no deception nor anything but the simple fact that, yes, this was his mission and his alone. He did this, the drone came from the *NN Drozir*, and he himself, as the captain, went ahead with this attempt to 'knock on their front door' on his own. What he did not think of nor consider was that the aliens might have visited their revenge on all the ships in front of them—rather than the drone alone. That I find to be a considerable lack of experience and judgment in a navy officer. But blame lies only at his feet—not with Novertag," she finished, and that put a silence over the room once more.

The admiral shifted in his seat. "If I was your admiral, you'd be court-martialed and sent to the brig," he said.

"In the Caliphate, your sentence would be longer and the lashes longer still," the Caliph added.

Heads nodded in the room, and the chairman called a halt to the discussion. "Then, for the record, we the executive committee of the RIM Confederacy Council find no blame to be assigned to our member, Novertag. However, we will include the minutes of this meeting when we turn over the captain to his ship under arrest and send him back to his realm. We also would like to thank the Master Adept for her ... her ... her adept ability and the fact that she was willing to share this as well with the committee. Kudos, ma'am," he finished off, and he slapped the tabletop as there appeared to be no gavels present. Not that he needed one, with such a small group, Tanner noted.

Going down the escalator, somehow the Master Adept ended up just one step above Tanner's spot, and she leaned forward to say very quietly in his ear, "Duke—could I ask that we meet in person

160

sometime in the next few days? I know that being a
Royal and now in charge of a six-planet realm is an
impossible task for many to even countenance. And
I'd like to talk to you, please, about these aliens—
can we agree to try to schedule that meeting ..."

He was looking out the huge windows on the
side off to his right, and he made no outward sign
he had heard the whispered query, but he nodded.

She patted him on the shoulder, and they went
down the escalator almost together.

Something is up, he thought, and that got him
another pat on the shoulder from the Master Adept.

#####

Major Stal was anything but slow. His forty-yard
dash was still a record standing from those years
ago at the Marine Academy on Neres. He wasn't as
good at hurdles as his big thighs were not meant to
be turned sideways as much as was considered
good form—but today, it didn't seem to matter.

Holding a series of combat readiness tests here on
Ghayth was always a good thing. Holding them at
the new naval base might have been better—but as
he was on station at the alien wreck in the far
southern continent, he'd simply adapted his
location to suit his needs.

He'd had the various pieces of equipment flown

161

in. There was an enormous wall with rope assists hanging from the top. Bit spools of barbed wire had been slowly uncoiled and stapled to the logs that had been freshly cut from the trees that lay near the beach. There were the standard sixty-pound packs, all exactly the same and oddly balanced, to provide a real burden on his men who were going to take the tests today.

He'd personally checked the five-mile course. It ran through the deep jungle on one side, across the sand bar that stretched out and into those woods from the beach, across two small creeks, and then, for a whole mile almost, it went upstream on the stream that had an uneven and rocky bottom.

While he had awarded the COR—Chief of Race—credentials to a lieutenant, he still took some pride as the course itself was going to be long at seven miles in total, challenging, and tough.

"Should make for some interesting times," he said to himself as he ran the pre-testing course himself. As he hoisted his leg once again, up and over the hurdles made from the foot-wide branches of the trees around the course and dragged into place, he grunted. *Good time up front in the crawl part, under the barbed wire for the two hundred yards. Check.*

He'd slowed a bit on the first run. The sand bar area, while only four hundred yards, was a real bitch to run on; the sand was so loosely packed that it was tough to try to run with any degree of speed. He'd bogged down, but then he knew all of the racers today would do the same, and he mentally checked off the next task on the course.

After that came the wall, and trying to spring from the sand at the wall's base was a non-working proposition. What he'd realized, as he'd jumped and had fallen five feet short each time, was that he —and the racers to follow—would need to adapt. He went off to the side of the large thirty-foot wall. He ran at it obliquely and then got two good footfalls on the wall itself as his hand stretched up and up. *Yes! I have the rope!* He quickly let his body swing with the lateral movement he'd just used, and then he twisted to face the wall and went up hand over hand on the rope to the top. He swung over and slid down the smooth side to the ground below. *That would make some of them frustrated, but if I can figure it out—so should they. Check.*

He sprung ahead. The pack on his back was still weighted more on the left side, and it rode on his left kidney badly, but he grinned as he jammed a hand beneath same and rubbed his scraped skin beneath the hard canvas bag. He used his right hand to hoist the right shoulder strap up a bit, and that got the bag a bit more off center, and he was able to bear the discomfort a bit easier.

"Five miles," he said to himself, and he settled into his quickest pace for that distance. Ahead of him, the course had been marked with dye, a nice bright orange color, to lead him and the racers to follow along the path.

First was the meadow before the woods as he left the wall and beach area behind him. He ran, his feet pounding on the grass, and he was careful to look ahead where each footstep would land. One thing he didn't want to do was to twist an ankle in a hole or an animal burrow.

At the end of the meadow, he turned as the dye markers showed to his left, and he followed a slowly dropping hill down to the bottom of a ravine. Huge trees—the xeno team had dubbed them mushroom trees because they looked like gigantic fifty-foot tall mushrooms, lay ahead, and some over the years, had fallen too. He picked his way the best that he could through the course, and after more than two hundred yards, he reached the bottom of the ravine.

He pounded right through the brook. He slipped a bit on one step. *Must mention to my COR that footing in water cannot be counted on. Check.*

He rose up the other side of the ravine, and the sounds of leaves and forest detritus crushed beneath his feet as he climbed the far side of the ravine. At the top, the orange markings led still

164

farther on to the left. He ran, keeping his attention on the course itself and nowhere else until a thunderous sound rising up from behind him distracted him, and the pain in his ears was actually sharp.

He grunted and clapped hands over his ears, but the sound did not dissipate at all. He slowed and as the sound behind him increased even more, he fell to his knees, shaking his head to try to rid himself of the pain of such a pure single note of painful sound.

He was unable to give himself even a small degree of comfort, and he knew his eyes were tearing up, and his ears—or maybe it was just his brain—were ringing so loudly in sync with that note that the resonance was almost more than he could stand.

He forced himself to stand, letting go of his ears, as the sound could not be blocked. He stumbled forward and turned around to face the alien wreck a couple of miles away from him on the beach. He broke into a trot to return.

Something had happened back there. His teeth were so clenched he had to breathe through his nose, and that was hard as he had trouble getting enough air to feed his muscles.

He knew he should count the number of steps he took to try to determine just how far 'out' he was from the wreck. After twenty-three steps, the sound stopped, and he collapsed in a heap in the dried leaves and undergrowth. He rolled over on his side, shook for a moment, and then forced himself up onto his knees. Sweat poured down his brow; more sweat than he'd generated from running the course so far. His muscles felt loose and yet shaky. His eyes were dry—he'd cried out more tears than he'd ever done before, and he nodded to himself as he took stock of his body.

"Able to stand. Check," he said to himself as he rose. "Able to walk, maybe to jog, back to the temporary marine tent base located beside the huge alien wreck. Check," he said, adding to his mental list as he began to walk and then jog.

As he moved toward the wreck, he continued to count the steps. At seven hundred and forty-six, he crested the rise to the right of the course below, and he jogged down the final hill to the beach and the wreck.

There had been some degree of competency. His second in command, Captain Pratt, was out in the field beside the large tent village where the marines were encamped at the wreck site. He was ordering some lesser ranks to carry out specific tasks, and Alver saw marines were already stationed on picket duty, each armed and at the ready. There were three personnel carriers lined up as well, and they held more marines ready to be dispatched should the need arise.

Good, he thought, *Pratt's on top of things.*

As he ran up and bent over, catching his breath, Captain Pratt acknowledged him and brought him up to speed. "Sir—glad to see you're okay. From what we know and have learned, twenty-one minutes ago, the wreck all of a sudden powered up —least that's what we're calling it. From inside in the rear, there was a sound—a huge single note of a hum—that was more than—well, Sir, more than most of us could stand. We have multiple casualties, Sir—all knocked out by that hum note.

"Just to let you know, that note was exterior only —the full xeno team and their small squad of marines inside the ship heard nothing. They were not affected at all—but they did pour out with the news that inside the ship, things were all of a sudden lighting up. Turned on, Professor Reynolds was shouting, the ship had been turned on.

"Out here, though, as we were mostly up at the testing course, which is about a mile thataway," Pratt said as he pointed back and to the left somewhat, "so the marines here were the ones that were badly affected. We have nineteen marines in sickbay, Sir—with as yet no diagnosis," he finished off.

Stal nodded. "Did any of you notice anything strange about that hum—that single note?" he asked.

His second in command nodded. "Yes, Sir. Blocking your ears didn't work—we all did that as soon as the hum note started. It was like in our brains rather than our ears."

Alver nodded. "Agreed. Let's get things in order, Captain. Cancel today's testing race, and send out a squad to go over the course in case we've some stragglers out there. I want a full roster audit too— who's missing if anyone. I want the surgeon over in sickbay to hustle through with that diagnosis—and if that means transport back to Neres and the Barony Hospital Ship, then so be it," he said.

He moved then with his aide, walking the paths between the tents looking for anything out of place.

Nothing.

He went to the big dining tent and saw the entire xeno team sitting there and drinking coffee. He sat with them and heard the same story. They'd been inside in one of the cargo bays when machinery, derricks, cranes, big display boards, and the like all were suddenly turned on. They'd not done it as they were having an argument, Reynolds admitted, about some item they'd found and its real and intended use.

They'd been shocked and had quickly run out of the cargo bay, across the whole ship, out the big entrance, and had assembled here since the incident. "No, we had not heard that hum or single note tone," Reynolds said, "but I assume it had something to do with the ship 'being plugged in all of a sudden.'"

Alver nodded. That made sense, but then if there was one thing he had long ago learned, anything alien can be anything—what made sense to one race might not be sensible to another.

He thanked Reynolds and let the xeno team know he was closing the ship to further entry by anyone and that he'd get back to the team when he had news.

He walked away toward the communications tent, and EYES ONLY messages were sent to Admiral Vennamo and the RIM Confederacy as well. While they were not a stakeholder here on Ghayth, it was still some kind of aggression—and with the alien ship up in orbit around Ghayth, Alver thought it prudent to send out notice as best he could.

"And now what's next?" he said to himself as he reached down to massage his left calf. "What's next?"

Niels Lofton, Leudie trade master, smiled at the Customs and Duties men as they approached, and he waited with his number two and the case at his feet.

They'd landed on Neen, the capital planet of the Duchy d'Avigdor just a half hour ago and had listed as their only unloads, a present for the new duke himself. That had made the normal rollout of the usual teams who greet every ship visiting Neen stop.

He had seen the motorized carrier on its way out to the landing pad that his ship, the *Tynes,* had dropped down on two hours ago, suddenly veer off from its direct path to the ship. It had swung into a big arcing turn and had returned to the administration building here on the landing port.

And they'd sat and waited, first up on the boarding deck on top of some cases that were being moved around. Then after an hour, when those cases had been taken away for their spots in a cargo hold somewhere, Niels and his aide walked down the ramp. The aide had been able to handle the wooden case easily.

Now, another hour later, that carrier had started up. Clambering down from the seats in the open vehicle, the Customs man moved forward; his yellow badging on his epaulets was easy to see. He was a man of about forty, and he had wavy brown hair and a big forehead lined with what Niels thought were stripes of his office.

He nodded to the aide, faced the captain of the

Tynes, and smiled. "We welcome you, Master Trader, to Neen. I understand that you have no cargo at all—inbound or outbound. Except, I understand, a present for the duke. A wedding present, perhaps a bit belatedly?" he asked.

Niels shook his head. "Not at all. I have the present right here in the case. Belts. Red metal belts —three of them—and I need to place them directly into the hands of the duke himself, I was told," Niels said.

The Customs man was smiling, but it was obvious after a half a minute, he was waiting for more.

"We assume that a gift for the duke would fall under the 'personal and private items' clause of the list of items that are both allowed and not charged any duty. Taxes. Nothing at all—but here is an extra thing to consider," he added as he took a half a step forward. "If you wish, you may certainly call out your Duchy d'Avigdor Provost guards to inspect the case—to look at the belts and make the decision if they—or rather you—think the duke should get his present from the Rulers of the Leudie Trading Rules group. It is from them that the gift comes—understand now?" he asked. Nicely. Very nicely.

The Customs man was in a bind, he knew, but as usual, when offered a way to save face, he took it like a drowning man seized a life ring. "Yes ... yes, that's exactly what I think we'll do. We'll provide you transport over to the ducal palace, arrange for them to know that you're coming—and the duke will greet you there in person if possible. We'll let these guards just check the case if we can ..." he said as he motioned for the two Provost guards to do his bidding.

They got down off the carrier and moved over to stand at the side of the group, and one bent to open up the case. He lifted out one of the red metal belts and looked it over. He twisted it and saw there were many red metal sections linked together. He checked the buckle but didn't touch it and then looked down into the case.

"Three belts, all look the same. No bombs, no poison, nothing that I can see would hurt our duke. Try it on," he said pointedly to the trader in front of him, which took them all by surprise.

Niels reached out to take the proffered belt and pushed it around his waist. Wearing the Leudie cloak meant he had to move the belt a little to fit, but he snapped the buckle together. *The belt is a simple ... well, a simple belt,* he thought and held out his hands, palms up, and that got nods all around.

"Three belts. We will allow this to pass inspection and be admitted to Neen—and yes," the Customs man said as he was making some notes on his tablet, "it fits under the personal and private items" clause as well. Let's get aboard, shall we?" he said.

In moments, they were motoring across the landing pads, whipping around an Alex'n freighter, two ship's chandlers coming out to service a Duchy Navy ship, and against the far end of the base, on pads all alone, two Barony warships.

That got a raised eyebrow; Niels knew about the latest items of news on the RIM. The alien presence over Ghayth was a big one but he'd heard no more than that.

The carrier left the gate with a wave from the Provost guard who was obviously in the loop. When the carrier got there, the bolster beam was up, and the Provost guard was saluting them by.

The salute was a bit unusual, Niels thought, but in less than ten minutes more, they were being saluted into the palace grounds, this time by a brace of four Provost guards.

Again, unusual, Niels thought as he clambered down.

"We will wait here," the Customs officer said, and from out of the palace doors ahead, down the stairs, came two navy officers—one a master sergeant, he noted.

"Trade Master Lofton, welcome. I have been sent to accompany you to the duke himself—and my corporal here will carry that case for you as well.

Gentlemen, please follow me," he said and turned, and they followed him. Behind them, the corporal carried the case, and Niels noted he carried it as if he expected it to explode.

Maybe it will, he thought, *maybe it will.*

They entered the huge doors that swung open to admit them, and after going across a part of the beautiful marble floor of the palace rotunda, Niels saw the doors closing behind them. Palace AI was aware of their presence, he knew, and that was fine too.

They walked down the rotunda, veering off to the left for a bit to curl around to their right. After walking underneath a staircase, they went down that lateral hallway. Even here in areas that were not so populated with the public, there was art on the walls—paintings, real oil paintings. Sculptures in recesses were also spotted here and there, and the rug on the floor was so thick that Niels imagined his shoes were sinking down inches into it.

The palace AI must have been watching their progress because at the end of the hallway, a solid wall in front of them disappeared. They continued to walk in an area that had been obviously kept in secure constraints. They walked. Not a word was said, and at the juncture ahead with a corridor that crossed their own, they took a left.

Niels could smell chlorine, which was odd.

At the second doorway ahead, the lead master sergeant opened the door, went a couple of feet more, and opened up an inner door as well.

The smell of chlorine grew stronger once the inner door was opened. Before him, Niels saw an indoor swimming pool complete with a wide and sunny deck off against the far windows. At the far end, what must be the shallow end of the pool, wide stairs rose up out of the pool.

Niels walked down the stairs leading to the pool's deck. *Deep end down here,* he thought. The surroundings were so overwhelming that a few minutes passed before he noticed the solitary swimmer in the pool doing laps across the width of the pool.

The length of the pool looked to be fifty yards and the width about half that. As Niels and the others walked down the deck alongside the pool , the swimmer never stopped. They reached a small grouping of chaise lounges and noted a robe draped over the back of one and a pair of sandals sitting there as well.

The duke is the swimmer and so we wait. Again, Niels thought, but he never let anything show on his face. Traders learned at an early age that to show your hand before it was called was just plain stupid trading. He smiled instead, stood like the others, and waited.

Niels counted nine more laps, and then the duke stopped at the edge of the pool facing away from them. He shook his head and jammed a little finger into one ear to try to worry out some water. He pushed off the wall as he turned to his left and moved down to the shallow end of the pool, climbing the stairs slowly and shaking his head to his right as though some water there just wouldn't drip out.

He turned the corner, saw his guests, and smiled as he walked right up to the two traders. "Trade Master Lofton—so good to see you again. Perhaps you might remember we met over on Halberd a few years back, before all that prison riot nonsense?" he said as he picked up a towel to dry himself.

Niels did remember meeting Captain Scott back then, but he was surprised the duke remembered. It had been a simple handshake at the welcome party the night before that nonsense—the prison riots that ended with the deaths of some of the rioters. As he remembered, Scott had killed some of same himself. *Nonsense indeed.*

"Duke. So very nice to meet you—again, Your Grace. Yes, I remember our previous meeting well, but this time, I come bearing gifts for you—from the ruling body on Leudie—the Leudie Trading Rules group," he said with all decorum.

The duke nodded. "Yes, Trade Master, and we know that you are the newest member of that group of thirty—really, heads of state all of you—and we hope that you have time to visit with us and spend some time with us too, for a real state visit."

"Um ... sadly, not at this time, Your Grace, but perhaps next time. As I said earlier, this time, I bring you a present. Might I ask that we perhaps limit the ears that hear what I have to say, as it's confidential, Your Grace."

The duke nodded and gestured, and the master sergeant and the corporal moved all the way back to the far stairs, went up same, and out of the pool room followed by the trader's aide.

They were now alone—the duke and the trader.

The duke looked at him. "Well, Niels, what is it?" he asked.

Diplomacy time is over, Niels thought, and he opened up the case and took out one belt.

"I bring you three of these belts. We got them inwards—almost three thousand lights inwards— about a year ago. From what we can tell and what we have tested, these are force field belts. We do not understand how they are powered, nor for that matter, more than turning them on and off," he said.

He doffed his cloak and put the belt on, and it stretched easily, the links expanding to fit it around him snugly. He reached down and behind the buckle to press the button that only appeared when the belt lay around a waist, and he clicked it to one side. Around Niels appeared a very faint glow or aura of golden mist.

"This makes the wearer invulnerable. We have tested it with every weapon that we have here on the RIM. Nothing can get through to injure the wearer of the belt. We have no idea how air gets through nor gravity for that matter either. You will pardon us though—we are traders and not lab gurus. And that is part of why we've decided to give these three to you," he said.

He clicked the button once more and handed the belt to the duke after he'd taken it off.

The duke took the belt and hefted it. He looked at it over and over as he turned it around in his hands. He paid particular attention to the buckle, but it offered up no secrets that he could see.

He held it in one hand and looked over at his guest. "So, Niels ... why me?"

The trade master nodded and spread his hands out in a wide gesture. "Your Grace—we know about the discovery of the alien anti-grav device and how it was discovered as one thing but it was modified and changed by you to become the drive itself. We know that you—or perhaps your team on the *Atlas*—were responsible, and we are hoping that you can help one more time.

"Help? Is there an issue that you have not told me?" he said.

He's quick, Niels thought, once again impressed with this Royal.

"Yes, not only does the belt lock out anything from getting in to harm the wearer—it also will not allow anything to leave the power belt shell either ..." he said.

The duke just looked at him. Then he gave a big nod. "Ahh ... which means that a simple robo-rifle, once trained on the wearer, will make that belt user not only invulnerable but also immobile. Without the ability to shoot at an attacker, the belt has little value. Might replace some guards at palaces, but that's all I see," he said, and Niels saw that he had captured the essence of the red power belt in that instant.

The duke fiddled with the belt's buckle some more. "So, you want me to see if I can deduce how this might be changed or modified to make it an offensive weapon too. Do I have that right?"

Bingo, Niels thought as he nodded. "Your Grace, you grasp what needs to be done, and we would ask that you share this with no one but we Leudies—the Leudie Trading Rules group—we, the Rulers," he said and waited.

The duke pondered that, and after a moment, he

179

replied. "I will not be able to keep this as confidential as non-lab folks might want. There will need to be a whole team assigned this, and that will mean that support services like logistics, purchasing, lab equipment and supplies, and, yes, even HR and personnel too will know that 'something is up.' But other than that, I will make a solemn ducal promise that I let no one else know. Not anyone on the RIM Confederacy Council, if that's what you're worried about."

Niels bowed his head and then nodded. "Agreed, Your Grace. We know that you will succeed, and that's not because of what happened back on Halberd or your climb in the Barony Navy or even your new dukedom. It's because you carry what we Leudies call the luck gene, where you are at the focus of major collisions between RIM Confederacy realms, technology, aliens—the gene makes you the focal point. It's what we believe, Your Grace. So this task should go to no one else, Your Grace," he said, and he bowed his head one more time.

The duke was taken aback, and for a minute or so, he stared at the Leudie trader in front of him. He looked like that idea was not so new to him— but then the added weight of the luck gene had added a wrinkle that had him stumped. Or baffled. Or confused.

He looked down at the belt and then at back at

Niels.

And he smiled. "Well then, I guess that I need to thank you and the Trading Rules group of Rulers. I do not know if that supposition is true or not. But I will accept the gift of the three belts and will take a real interest in the testing of same. I will also, if you allow me to, contact you directly via EYES ONLY Ansible with any news. Will that be acceptable, Trade Master?"

Niels grinned at him.

"Absolutely, Your Grace. And might I add that this luck gene is well known on Leudie and other realms here too. If it were possible, Your Grace, I'd make you my own first mate—but alas, you're human," he said.

Around his collar, his neck snake had chosen this moment to stretch and swivel its location on the Leudie's neck, and he reached up to move it to a more comfortable position and that took a second.

The duke nodded and walked with him all the way down the long side of the pool, to the stairs, and up and out to the palace proper.

Moments later, as the carrier pulled away with Trade Master Lofton and his aide, the Customs officer made pleasantries and chatted about Neen and what a great season it was for a visit and how so many Leudies arrived, unloaded, then loaded up, and went away without really learning about the planet.

Niels smiled as he listened, but his real thought was about the duke and the belts; he wondered what the outcome of this gift might be. What he was sure of was that the Duke d'Avigdor had the luck gene. *What that would mean would be of great interest...*

CHAPTER SIX

The Duchess d'Avigdor was still a bit confused, but then that sometimes went along, as she well knew, with trying to learn exactly how she was to get around here in the new duchy palace. Walking with two aides—top aides, she'd been told these two were—meant she was slowly trying to catch on to where and what each of the almost six hundred rooms in the palace were. At least that's what she'd been told when they left the residential area up on the fourth floor of the palace.

So far, they'd walked the big rotunda with all of the corridors and hallways branching off. She had gone trooping down one after another, entering room after room to take a look around and making notes on the list on her tablet. Some, she realized, were rooms that were well past their "best-before date" and would need her attention to upgrade the décor. In some cases, the old windows that looked out on the palace grounds needed to be replaced. So far, by her reckoning, there were nineteen of these rooms, and she was aware they had not even completed ten percent of the total list of rooms.

She nodded at the one aide, the tall young man, who was pointing out that yes, once again, this room had the older window styles, and one of them even had some water staining way up at the top. "Needs repairs, I would think, Ma'am," he said, his finger poised over his tablet.

She nodded and said, "Agreed, get this done up at the top of the list."

He made some clicks on his keyboard, and they left the medium-sized salon to go back out to the hallway. Once again, they turned to their left to move to the next room.

It was room after room, and Helena wondered how long it would take to go through every room. Most didn't need much. Some that were on the other side of the hallway, facing the front of the palace, had been refurbished in the past decade or so. Those rooms had new windows, paint, and carpets, and she noted a few—only a few—of those stuffed heads from hunting trips that the dukes had so enjoyed.

As she stepped on the escalator to go up to the

second floor, she shook her head. Thank God, the new duke was not much into hunting. Never mind that he was on Anulet right now with some of his groomsmen doing exactly what she thought was a good thing to do—to bring them together—but surely there might have been something else rather than hunting?

She sighed. *Probably not. Men—men from every walk of life, from every world—seemed to enjoy the hunt. Part of their genes,* she thought. *So, it was a good thing, maybe,* and at the top of the escalator, the taller aide directed her to the left side first.

It, like the three-hundred-foot-long major corridor down one floor, stretched out for the same distance, and she could see doorway after doorway. She sighed. *More rooms and more to come.*

"Ma'am, this area ahead on the front side of the building, we—well the staff here at the palace—have taken to call this area the colored-world collection."

And as they walked into the first room on the left, she learned why. Green. Everything in the room was green or a shade or tint of same. Carpet. Walls. Tapestry on the wall. Window frames. There were seven groupings of green upholstered couches and wing chairs, and the green wood was polished and very shiny for all of the tables as well. Lamps standing on some of the end tables had green

185

shades, and she was sure, if they turned one on, the light would be green as well.

She looked at the other aide, the shorter woman, and said, "And the rationale behind doing this— tones of a single color were ...?"

She nodded first, and then she looked down at her own tablet, swiped a few pages to one side, and then looked up. "Ma'am, there is no reason that we have on file, as to why this was done—and there are twenty-nine of these rooms in a row, Ma'am—each with its own color," she said.

Her voice, Helena could tell, was a bit apologetic but there was no blame as to why she didn't have an answer. "Can you at least identify who did this?" she asked.

The aide nodded and pointed at her tablet screen. "Yes, Ma'am, that is recorded in the palace database. It was done by—they all were done, all of the twenty-nine rooms—by the Duchess d'Avigdor that preceded you. That is the late duke's mother, Ma'am. She seemed to have entered no rationale, but the rooms were all done about the same time, Ma'am, about eighty years ago," she finished off.

Helena nodded as they left the green room, and she only glanced in the rest of colored rooms. She couldn't believe the orange room. The black room was a room she would never enter, and yet the lavender room looked so lovely.

"Fine, please note for me on the list that I will discuss the future of these 'colored-world' rooms with the palace designer. Please make that meeting, say, for the day after tomorrow. Colored-world collection indeed," she said, her voice resonating with a confused tone.

As they went on, she made the hypothesis that the last duke, David, had done little about the palace. He'd lived in it for his whole life, and it had remained, as she was learning, just like his mom and dad had left it.

There was more too. She was a bit surprised at one doorway that had a triple set of doors going into same. The last set opened, and all she could smell was some kind of irritating odor. Inside the huge room was a wall of some fine fencing. Birds lived behind the fencing. Birds of all colors and kinds. What must have been a hundred birds lived in the palace on the second floor in an indoor aviary.

Some came over at their entrance by flying—but then she looked down at the edge of the enclosure in the room. Some had, well, rolled over. "Unusual gait," she said to herself as another one came out of the well-pruned set of shrubs. It was a bird, or at least she thought it was. It had a feathered body and head—bright yellow in color mostly though there was some green there too. But the feet—or what should have been feet—were the interesting thing. Instead of two gripping feet on legs, a scaled ball that was wider than it was tall with the legs on each side acted somewhat like axles. As the yellow bird leaned forward, that movement made the ball of scaled skin or hide rotate to move the bird ahead. As she watched, she noted that the birds could control the movement of their ball so closely that they were able to jockey for position and move about quite easily.

She looked at the aides. "And that's one hell of an unusual-looking bird," she said, her voice wondering.

"They're called ball birds—at least that's what the database calls them ... they're from a world in Pentyaan space, and there are more than a dozen in there," the tall aide said.

She looked back at the aides, and she pointed at the tall one this time but said not a word.

"Umm ... yes, Ma'am. Perhaps we should have warned you, but again, the mother of the late duke liked birds. So this room was built, and they imported birds from around the RIM Confederacy. They live and reproduce, and we're told that she used to love going into the aviary and sitting with them, and she'd feed them and pet them. At least that's what the palace database says, Ma'am."

He looked a bit pained at this. *Surely*, she

thought, *this is perhaps a bit embarrassing, but then again Royals will be Royals.*

"What other rooms lying ahead do you think I'll be surprised at? Can you tell me that?" she said calmly.

He swiped on his own tablet a few times and tilted it so the other aide could see. She nodded at something as she pointed at the screen, and then he looked up at her.

"Ma'am, yes, there are a couple of what we might call as oddball items. One is the trophy room up on the third floor—more than three hundred mounted trophies—all from previous dukes and their hunts. Some of the duchesses, who have come to be same, have tried to get rid of that room—but it's always been kept, Ma'am. Then, there's the realm rooms— each is totally designed and decorated for each of the duchy realm planets ... Dover and Waterloo, et cetera, Ma'am. Some are ... well, some are a real head shake, Ma'am, but they are probably needed as each head of state of each of our realm planets visits his own each time they come to the duchy palace, Ma'am."

At least there's no room with snakes or Jaels or even Tanalorgs ... and how bad can the realm world rooms be anyways? She nodded and then they left the aviary room.

"Any idea how many of the six hundred or so

rooms in the palace have more than one door?" Helena asked.

He clicked some on-screen buttons, paused, and then clicked the same buttons she noted. "There are seven rooms that have more than a single door, Ma'am."

She nodded. Seven rooms with more than one door meant that these seven rooms had to keep odors captured. She groaned. *I can't wait.* She wished Tanner could have been with her to see some of this, but then he was off hunting. She hoped he was safe.

·

Off Ghayth, the *Exeter* lay in orbit within a hundred miles of the alien ship that still was dormant. "But dormancy does not mean non-threatening," Captain Magnusson said to himself, and he nodded to the helm.

They, too, had been greeted by the usual ultra-bright teal ray, which had flicked into existence to shine on the *Exeter* and then went out.

"Take us in closer, Helm ... but keep us at least twice as far away from the ship as their force field extends. No sense in causing any kind of upset feelings," he said.

The *Exeter* had moved to Ghayth at his command. He had wanted to see the ship himself, and when they'd popped out of subspace, they had been recognized by the *Wilson*, the Ghayth space station, and had acknowledged they were just there on a fact finding mission, as the Ansible officer had been coached to say.

He also told them that he carried an EYES ONLY from the Baroness to Commander Williams, the head Barony Navy man on the planet. Magnusson nodded to his Ansible officer and the message—printed out—was sealed in a diplomatic pouch and sent off via shuttle to the *Wilson* for them to relay down to the planet.

That got silence from the station, and then a "Roger" back to them.

As the *Exeter* was in the same navy as the *Wilson*, there was no reason for any kind of worries, the administrator on the space station must have thought, and the *Exeter* was free to move about wherever it needed to.

Up here in orbit, the captain noted, there were only two other ships currently.

The *Atlas*, the huge supra-destroyer, the largest ship in the Barony Navy—in any navy on the RIM —lay off to port. He knew that the captain, Karl Sheldon, had recently been appointed as the latest captain, Kondo Lazaro, had followed the same path as his predecessor, Tanner Scott, and had moved up to bigger and greater things.

Don't know about the real sense in having a science officer take over the captain's chair, Magnusson thought, *but one thing was for sure—the Atlas would never make any science mistakes out here.*

The only other ship was a Faraway trader, which was in the process of off-loading some cargo to a small cargo shuttle. The job was just about over, and sure enough, as the *Exeter* moved slowly past, the shuttle blasted off and dove around the *Exeter* and headed down toward Ghayth.

Mel watched the shuttle as it zoomed by and then noted the flares from the starboard side of their engines as the ship veered south—way south to point well beyond the equator.

"Helm," he said, "trace that shuttle, and let me know where it ends up, will you?"

The affirmative response back to him was quick, and still, he wondered why the shuttle would be aiming so far south when all the Ghayth civilization lay in the northern continent. *Only way to know is to see where this shuttle goes. Cargo,* he thought. *Must ask what that was in a way that won't matter to anyone else.*

He grinned. "Things are already full of fact finding fun," he said to himself, and he watched up on the big view-screen as the *Exeter* slowly moved in a large circle a few miles wide of the alien ship.

Big, he thought. *Long—least a mile long—with that*

huge disk in the middle. The disk holds the aliens. I have no idea what the long tapering top and bottom tubular areas are for. At least not yet.

"Vids running?" he inquired, and the reply from his science office behind him affirmed that was a fact too.

So, the aliens lie here and wait. Force field keeps all of us at bay. Even the nuke he'd heard about via RIM scuttlebutt not only had not done a thing to the alien ship, but it had made the drone ship disappear. No explosion. No metal dripping from lasers, energy pulse weapons, or plasma cannons. Nothing but a simple blink, and the drone ship was gone.

That technology proved to him that these aliens were superior—at least in the weapons area.

As the *Exeter* slowly finished the circle around the alien ship, he was satisfied; he'd seen enough.

There was nothing to be done about the alien ship. They'd talk when they were ready.

His console beeped and a map of the southern continent, the big one to the west, showed up on his screen, and it appeared that the cargo shuttle had made landfall. On the edge of the big southern sea and the continent, it had set down. He had no idea why and for what purpose that cargo was needed.

"For tomorrow," he said to himself, and then he told his helmsman to take her out of orbit and back to Neres City to the navy base. "More than enough time for that ..."

He smiled as he got the EYES ONLY received message from Commander Williams directly on his own captain's console. He knew what was on the message—from today, all ships coming to Ghayth would be required to land directly on the planet itself down at the landing port on Base-1. This, he had pointed out to the Baroness, would keep that alien intruder ship alone up in space with the *Wilson* space station and the three other ships there —the *Atlas*, the *Newton*, and the *Connecticut*.

All Barony Navy ships were on guard, flanking the intruder ship.

All three were on alert status, watching and never blinking away from the aliens.

#####

"Caliph, may I present the Enkian ambassador, Eecesoe Qig," his aide said as the Caliph was lounging in his study. Normally, he'd have taken the meeting in one of the offices areas of the palace tents, but today, he'd decided he needed to show the Enkian that he was trivial in the grand scheme of things. What better way to do that than by lounging on a couch while the ambassador stood in front of him.

"He'd soon learn who was boss here," the Caliph

said to himself, and he nodded to his aide to show in the Enkian.

Short—perhaps especially so from the Caliph's point of view as he stood six feet, six inches—the Enkian was about five feet and maybe an inch or two tall as were all Enkians. He had a beak instead of lips and feathered tips on his toes above the big talons that perhaps had been used eons ago to kill prey. The ambassador wore a short brown jacket with the same red and blue coloration as a logo of the Enkian's muse.

On top of his head, the feathered crest of mixed red and blue feathers signified this Enkian belonged to the Enkian group known as the Fine Arts Muse. It had been this Enkian's job to negotiate the original agreement with the Caliphate—and to accept the position within the Caliphate realm as a subject planet—in exchange for FTL. That was a technology the Enkians had never discovered, and with the addition of the new Barony Drive, one could be anywhere on the RIM in seconds.

And part of being a subject planet of the Caliphate meant they would be a welcome partner in all things—and the thing the Caliph had bargained for the mining rights to the Xithricite, the red metal ores from the meteorite that was found on Enki. It was a small item and had been hidden among so many other items that both Enki and the

Caliphate would share and also use for trading items too.

"Hidden. But most important," the Caliph said to himself, knowing the recent shipment of new huge forges from Roor to Neria had enabled their own new foundries to be able to smelt and generate new Xithricite panels for their ships. "What, four ships now?" he asked himself as the door closed behind the aide.

"Ambassador Qig, please do come in," he said as he slid up a bit on the couch, keeping his legs still outstretched on the cushion beside him. *Subtle, perhaps...but obviously, it shows that as I am this man's Caliph, the respect he gets is at a minimum.*

Ambassador Qig leaned over at the waist and gave a very formal bow. *Good,* Sharia thought, *he knows protocol, and my show of no respect does not influence him at all.*

"May I say, Caliph, that it is so nice that you could receive me at such short notice. I thank you for that—Enki, in fact, thanks you—for the quickness to grant our meeting request," he said.

The Caliph nodded. *Nothing to say means that he will keep on talking, and that's what we want.*

Ambassador Qig looked around, and the Caliph could see him taking in what was obviously not a meeting room. A couch and three chairs were spread out to one side braced by a huge cast bronze table that held a pile of magazines—real paper magazines, which were quite old—a tablet flashing some icon, a riding crop, and a helmet that one might wear on an open carrier or a motorcycle perhaps. A pair of gloves was wadded up beside those items too. In the far corner, a fireplace that had a very low flame on was gently wafting warmth across the tented room. There was no art on the walls, but he could see, the Caliph noticed, that there were view-screens posted in a whole bank of same along one canvas wall.

He still looked at the Enkian, one eyebrow now atilt.

"If it please the Caliph, I come to you today—after lengthy discussions with the other four Muse groups on Enki—and we have a request to make, if you'd consider same?"

Ah, so that is how he wishes this to go, the Caliph thought. *Standing flat-footed—well, flat-taloned might be a better way to describe it—and ready for any kind of an answer. And so he will get one.* "Ambassador—as a subject planet of the Caliphate—we do not discuss requests as you put it. Instead, one normally just makes same through your own channels to our Realm Subject Ministry, and they handle same. Follow me, Ambassador?"

The ambassador squirmed just a teensy bit—or maybe he was just shifting his weight on those long talons that were carefully being managed by the Enkian to not pierce the canvas floor. "Caliph, but this is a private item that we do not—did not think —it should be sent through our normal channels— good as they are, Caliph," he said as he nodded vigorously.

Brown-nosing now, Sharia thought but he didn't speak.

"Caliph, I have come to speak to you about the mining rights that the Caliphate has with us—and the red metal known as Xithricite," he said.

There it is, the Caliph thought. *Time to drill down on his issue.* "And what, can we ask, is the problem? Are we taking too much, or are we not repaying for what we take with our own resources as payment," he asked nicely.

The ambassador waved both of his feathered hands back and forth. "No ... no, Caliph. We are more than happy with the mining rights and its trade deal—but it's that we have only recently found out what the red metal ... well ... what it is, Caliph. And that's why I'm here."

And quiet once more, the Caliph noted, as the ambassador awaited a response. Sharia did not reply as he reached for the glass of juice beside him on the end table at this end of the couch he reclined upon.

"Caliph, the red metal—this Xithricite, as you call

198

it—has a special property. It appears that, after our testing, that it is impervious to all kinds of weaponry that works thermally. That is, heat from a laser or an energy pulse weapon or a plasma cannon—all new to us Enkians, of course, but common here on the RIM —cannot penetrate the metal. It seems to just wisp away any kind of thermal attack. We did note that, depending on the thickness of the red metal panels, a simple rifle shot will pierce it easily, so the metal is not a perfect shield. But we wanted you to know that as soon as our own Resources Muse came up with these answers after we began testing the red metal ourselves."

They have the reason why the Xithricite has value, that's not so good, the Caliph thought.

"And do I take it that now that this is a known item for the red metal, that you wish to renegotiate the deal we made with you? Is that it, Ambassador?" he asked.

The ambassador just nodded. He couldn't even say out loud that he was here to work out a better deal for Enki.

The Caliph took another big sip out of his tall glass of juice. As usual, the sweet and sour quaff tasted good. "Then let me right up front say no. We have a deal, Ambassador—one that Enki both negotiated and signed as they became a realm of the

Caliphate. There will be no renegotiation at all, Ambassador. The only thing I can offer is that you have the right, as a subject planet of the realm, to go to the RIM Confederacy Council, apply for independent status to leave the Caliphate as a subject planet. While, if memory serves, that takes a year or two, you would end up exactly as you were before we ever came to Enki. Alone. On your planet with no FTL, no Caliphate ships or oversight, and more importantly, no protection from anyone else here on the RIM either. That is the only thing you can do—or you can let our deal stand."

While he'd been talking, the Caliph noted that the ambassador had been straightening up in his posture, almost now at attention, and his beak had been squared away. On top of his head, those large crested red and blue feathers had been pulled down and back and they were nowhere near the height they had been.

The ambassador nodded to the Caliph and said, "As the Caliph wishes, we will not ask for any further renegotiation at this time." He then bowed slightly from the waist, turned, and strode out of the room.

"Went well," the Caliph said. When faced with what it would cost them to drop out of the Caliphate, the ambassador had folded his tent and sped off in the night.

"Juice is good," he said, "must have some more." He lay back down to rest. Being the Caliph was a worrisome experience—no two ways about that. He sighed as he crossed one long, long leg over the other, and with a forearm over his eyes, he said, "Couch appreciation time" to himself and settled in for a nap.

About ten feet away, on the spot where Ambassador Qig had been standing, and unnoticed by him, there were holes in the tent floor from the Enkian's talons which had been gripped so tightly they'd gone right through.

She hadn't found much help—any really—in the huge Praix tome that had been in the Issian race's hands for twenty centuries. She didn't think there would be anything that might actually point her at an answer to help her in her quest for knowledge. She had spent more than a solid day, again, flipping pages and seeing notes on other races, other worlds, and other galaxies, and that was just a blur to her ... there was nothing there.

She had spent a few hours just staring out the windows from her quarters here in the high tower. There was little to see, but she did note that on the abandoned farm just outside the walled city, something was happening on the road. A truck sat there, and there were a couple of men out in the close field, just beyond the rail fence. The men were trimming the roughly overgrown weeds and growth. They'd already cleared a few yards, and the growth of branches and weedy shrubs no longer hid the rails in that spot.

Above, she saw a raptor floating, and she thought it was looking for lunch. It hung in the updrafts as it slowly tilted one way and then the other. But it didn't find a reason to dive for prey in the few minutes she watched; it floated above all the land below, as if it was above all for a reason.

She nodded at that suddenly apropos thought—above all for a reason. Like the Praix. Above all included not only the RIM Confederacy but the whole of the Milky Way Galaxy. And the reason was what she needed to find ... and how to get that reason undone.

She'd also talked to her aides. In fact, she'd called them all in for a meeting and had asked them to consider a hypothetical. And after explaining her conundrum, she asked them for counsel.

One of the aides she saw little of asked if the hypothetical she had posed to them—that one very superior race was asking for a lesser race to join them, but that would mean they would be slaves to the superior race—was it really a true thing?

She had by her nature, hidden her own mind and the real truth. But she wavered. And then she remembered that the Praix had skills in the mind reading area that were as good as the Issians—it was going to be over soon if too many people knew. It wasn't that she didn't trust her aides or any Issians other than her inner circle, but she knew that the fewer who knew, the better.

So she had lied, and she had done it well. Not real at all, she'd said.

The aide had nodded and provided her opinion. The aide had suggested the superior race should be reasoned with and the lesser race should not be a part of any slave society. All dressed in the traditional Issian black robes with the large medallion necklace, the dozen men and women attending the meeting had nodded and confirmed they shared the same opinion.

That had been yesterday too, and she had thanked them all. And today, she was as stumped as ever. She had no idea why the thought came to her.

It certainly was not anything she'd been thinking of—nor for that matter had anything made her think of this—it was more of a sudden insight that came to her out of the blue as they said on some human planets.

The duke. He was, without any arguments from

any Issian, one of the focus points around which the future of the RIM Confederacy was levered by the man. Her previous Master Adept had spoken to her many times of Tanner and how time after time, the events that spun around him were the ones that shaped their futures all over the RIM. She thought that through, and her head began to nod as she ran through the list.

He had been so much an important part—the crux, really—of the prison riot on Halberd, and he had saved all the attending heads of state on the RIM prison planet.

Via that involvement, he had been one of the reasons Olbia had fought for its independence from the Caliphate.

He had been part of one of the small groups who had found the Praix anti-grav devices—which had led to the release of the Barony Drive that had changed travel in the RIM. FTL had become almost instant at his hand as these ancient relics still had life in them.

He had been the one on the Hospital Ship who had done his own personal vac jump out into space to kill the thief who had tried to steal the Ikarian virus vaccine. The fact that happened allowed the Baroness to roll out the vaccine to the whole of the RIM Confederacy realms.

He had been on the task force that had taken on

the alien invaders, the reapers, as they'd been called, on Memories and had come up with the plan that had worked to destroy them—his Chicken Kiev defense, he had called it.

She thought about how he had worked wonders on Eons, just fifty miles from here, when he'd helped to get the RIM Naval Academy built and open on time. Now, more that 2,500 new graduates were coming out annually. All of the side effects of that, the publicity of the twins and the Tavira labs, had faded into oblivion. Of that, she was personally happy.

His own wedding had been a horrendous event with her predecessor, the late Master Adept, and the Duke d'Avigdor both killed by Tanner's own sister. He was also looking after her future too.

And lastly, he had been more than a part of the future of the Duchy d'Avigdor when he'd accepted the inheritance of the ducal crown and had taken over their six-planet realm.

Surely, the appearance of the Praix over Ghayth was an item that in his hands would mean a better ending for the RIM as a whole, she thought, finally arriving at a possible solution. *Surely, that might mean the Praix could be, at the least, driven off and, at the best, destroyed.*

As the thought of somehow bringing this all to the duke played out in her head, she was sad now that she could not call on Bram to help—to guide the duke into this task.

Or ... might I be able to do just that ... she thought. As she began to work on that thought, the hawk still soared above the farm below as she went back to the window. While her eyes were older, she could certainly see what the men who'd been working on the property had done. Attached to the railing was a large sign, and even from here, she could see it read FOR SALE.

Interesting, she thought. For some reason, the farmer—or maybe, more truthfully, his bank—had put up a sign to sell the farm. She wondered about that and knew she'd have to read the latest climate change reports, but more than that, she had to focus on how to get to the duke and gain his help ... to save the RIM Confederacy.

CHAPTER SEVEN

"Getting the call out to the Roma captain had been the first step in working out answers to the sudden rebirth of the Ghayth wreck," the Baroness said to herself. She'd had an aide EYES ONLY on her behalf to the *Jamison,* and she had called the woman to the baronial palace to meet up.

She swirled the wine glass—you were supposed to she'd been told nicely by her new sommelier, as that made the wine aerate more which increased the bouquet. At least that's what she'd been told at the last tasting led by the Quaran who ought to know wines.

She sniffed. It smelled like wine. She took a little sip, sucked in air from tightened lips, and then swallowed. "Yup, it was wine," she said to herself as she then took a big gulp of same.

At the side of this small salon, an EliteGuard came in and said, "Baroness, the Roma captain is without."

She nodded, put down the wine glass, sat up straighter, and said, "Bring her in."

The EliteGuard replied, "Yes, Ma'am." He saluted and a moment later, Captain Daika Rossum walked in and strode over to sit opposite her.

Captain Rossum was typically dressed in the fashion of her race—the leather boots and vest over forest brown and green leggings and a top that was tight over her breasts. Her long curly tresses hung over her shoulders, and the Baroness noted that the icon of those two cogs and the hammer were still front and center over her chest.

She leaned back and pointed at her own glass of wine, thinking it never hurt to be friendly. "Would you care for a glass of wine perhaps, Captain?"

Daika nodded agreement, and the palace AI noted same. In moments, a steward brought in a fresh glass of the same red wine the Baroness was already drinking. She accepted the glass, took two big swallows, and put the glass down.

The Baroness bypassed the remaining social niceties. "Captain, we have an issue over on Ghayth. It's not public knowledge, so this may be somewhat surprising to you, but there is an alien wreck there, and we've been working with a xeno team to find out more. More about their technology, their ship, and, yes, if there are alien artifacts there that we can use. Perhaps you know the story of the Barony Drive and how it came from initial finds on Ghayth," she said.

Daika nodded and asked a question. "Baroness, may I ask—how long ago was the wreck found?"

"Almost two years now," the Baroness replied as she sipped the red wine, trying to use her taste buds to savor the vintage, as she went on.

"And it's over Ghayth that the alien ship—the intruder, I believe, is what the vid press is calling them—hangs as well. Still nothing new there, it's behind its force fields at rest. But there was a major change with regards to the wrecked ship just two days ago.

"It was somehow, and from somewhere, turned on. That is, it came to life—all the ship now is powered and up and running but still a wreck that we can enter and walk within. And that's the issue," she said, downing the last of her glass of wine. She put it down and waved at the AI so there would be no more interruptions.

The Baroness continued. "In two years, we've learned very little. In two years, we've made little headway in learning the secrets of the wreck. Our xeno team, the best in the Barony, has made some interesting small discoveries—but not enough and not soon enough. Which is why I've called you in." She leaned forward and pointed at the captain. "I want you—and whomever you deem needed—to go to Ghayth and look over this wreck. With your inherent scavenging skills and knowledge—far and away outside what we know here on the RIM—you might find something quicker and easier. We require that this be a top-secret mission by you, but you will have full powers once on the wreck to do as you want. All I want is results," she said.

"Results, Ma'am? Like real knowledge or science that we can take from the wreck?" the captain posed.

"Exactly," she said and smiled. "The wreck may well be a part of the same aliens as the intruders that now lie off Ghayth. Or not. Or perhaps the intruders are there to also use the wreck in ways we don't as yet understand. But we want you to shortcut them and the xeno team too. I want answers, Captain—and as your Baroness, I command it," she finished off.

The captain just stared back for a moment. Her eyes were locked on the Baroness's eyes, and then she looked down at her wine glass still held in a hand on her lap. She nodded and drained the glass in one gulp. "Baroness, it will be my privilege to go to Ghayth on this mission for you and to find out what we can," she said.

The Baroness nodded, and with a flick of her head, the EliteGuard once more entered the room and held the door open for the captain to leave. "But do be careful," she added, "alien technology is an unknown."

A bit trite but at least I'm showing some degree of concern. Some ... She waved at the AI, which constantly monitored her all over the barony palace, and a new glass of red wine was brought in for her.

"Now," she said once more, "swirl the glass to help the bouquet ... this being a Baroness is not so hard ..."

#####

The talks now had been going on for over an hour. CWO Hartford, a Barony Navy noncommissioned officer who Tanner had asked for from the Barony, had been assigned to him here on the Duchy d'Avigdor naval base on Neen. He'd been here all of four days, and they had no answer. Judging from the look on his face, an answer might never present itself.

Tanner nodded. He was way past his understanding of the physics Hartford was trying to impart to him. "Wait ... okay ... I think I have an inkling of what you're trying to say. Is it that because the belts are powered from we don't know where that is the major issue?"

Hartford nodded but did let out a sigh at the same time.

Here, in the secure labs down in the basement of the navy administration building, locked behind the huge rack of vaulted doors, the testing had been going on for those four days.

Four days ago, he'd nicely brought the chief up to speed on the belts and his acquiring same from the Leudies. He did admit he had little real background as to why he'd been chosen to find an answer to the belt problems, but that was for another day.

He had passed along what little he knew and then had given the chief a green light. "Do whatever you need to do—to see if we can make the belts both a defensive and offensive weapon."

Upon being charged with that duty, Hartford had grinned. "I'm on that, Your Grace." With a deep bow, he had taken the three belts and had begun his testing.

First, Tanner had heard, he had checked on the truthfulness of the belt's abilities. Hartford had donned one himself. He'd learned how to turn it on and then off. Then, he'd had a Provost guard assigned to the labs use his needler first on the lowest setting to see if it was capable of breaching the belt's shield. The needler had not breached the shield, nor had the belt allowed the needler to hurt him at all—all the way up to a lethal dose of needler rays.

They'd also tried a blaster, which had not gotten through. A Colt and a Merkel had been tried too, but the bullets had simply hit the glow of the belt at its extremities and had dropped on the floor. They'd tried every single kind of offensive small arms and nothing had made any dent in the belt's abilities.

Hartford had then known he was working from what he knew to be true. He'd started from that premise and had first thought about natural forces. He had wondered how long one could stay in a belt. He'd questioned if oxygen somehow got through the belt's shields or if there was a limit on how long one could breathe in same.

He'd tested the belt using a water tank over in the wave action center—what that was doing as a part of the navy labs was beyond any question.

And, it had seemed that the belts could be turned on and the wearer could stay in same for at least a full day—much longer than what had been thought. The Provost guard who had tested the belt by being immersed in the water had proved the belt was not allowing any air to be sucked into the belt's interior of the shield. Air was being provided by something else.

That had Hartford stumped for a whole day. But it had answered what had been a worrisome problem. If air was allowed inside the belt shield, one could simply send a cloud of gas that could poison the belt wearer.

Just yesterday, Hartford had looked at natural forces. He'd taken a shuttle out with a group of other lab scientists and some Provost guards too. They'd gone about two thousand miles north by northwest to a long ridge of rough and tumble mountains. There, they'd set up shop and tested the belt shield by having a rockslide come down on top of a belt wearer. It had been hard to arrange it so that it could be tested, but after a couple of false starts, a Provost guard was covered in scree. He'd simply walked out of that covering of the rock rubble—the rocks moving out of his way as he walked.

Hartford had made many notes on that. The fact that a one-hundred-ninety-pound Provost guard could simply walk ahead and the rocks in front of him moved, rolled, and fell away from his path was one thing. However, he had been unable to find any relationship between inertia and momentum and the belt itself. The tendency of an object to resist changes in its state of motion varied with mass, and the mass of the rocks had been much more than the mass of the Provost guard.

Tanner sighed. *It is physics,* he thought, *and while it's important—for someone in a lab coat—all I want is results.*

And today, they'd been looking at the physics only. No testing. No Provost guards. Not a belt had been turned on. Instead, they sat in a meeting. Tanner, Hartford, and two of his top lab guys, Tanner thought, were there to talk about where they were.

Hartford began reviewing the final facts. "We still do not know where the power comes from. But one thing we do know is that the belts appear to be somehow—and this is a reach I know—somehow not a part of 'now.' There is no other explanation, that we can come up with."

He held out a finger on his six-digit hand and ticked off the first thumb. "One, the belt prevents anything from entering the space of the wearer of the belt."

He ticked off the first finger. "Two, we know that the belt somehow does not pass oxygen through the shield to the wearer of the belt. Proved by the underwater testing. The Provost guard was able to breathe for the full twelve hours he was on the bottom of that wave pool. One other thing we learned was that unlike the normal leaching of warmth—from an immersed body to the water itself —he reported back afterwards that there was no chill or coldness at all. This is a known result from cold water immersion and hypothermia factors."

Hartford paused and looked at Tanner. When there was no reply, he ticked another finger. "Three, the belt appears to not have a wide swath around the wearer. That is, the belt appears to set up a shield around the wearer that is only one inch larger than the person wearing the belt. Carrying in, say, a broom, which we did test, puts the same shield around the broom when it's held in the belt wearer's hands."

He ticked his fourth finger off. "Four, if something from the belt wearer is dropped ... and the wearer moves on, that item is no longer within the belt shield protection area. It means that the belt wearer can drop items, but they lose their invulnerability."

He ticked his last finger. "The belt wearer cannot add anything to the belt shield's protection area. If the belt wearer approaches something and tries to pick it up—the shield prevents him from doing that. Once started, the belt is prohibitive of being enlarged."

He ticked his second thumb on his hand. "All of which leads us to the final issue—how can we allow the belt wearer to add an offensive role to the belt's abilities?" He squeezed his hand into a fist. "And so far, Your Grace, we are at a loss. We have no idea as yet—but we do have a solid grasp of the belt and its capabilities."

#####

As the sand dune rose, Tanner gunned the cycle, and she climbed the hill beautifully. At the top of the crest, the winds were now no longer in his face, and behind him, he could hear the roar of the Caliph's bike as it came up after, him but it sounded like he was falling behind.

Tanner grimaced as the bike crested the dune, and below the drop away was almost a sixty-degree slope. He twisted the bars to the left just a bit, and the momentum took him up and over the knife-edge of the dune. As he began to roll down the slope, the bike veered left. As he slowly pressed down with his right foot on the rear brake, he leaned more and more to his left as the rear twin wheels began to drift to the right. Sliding like this, he knew, was a lesson in how to have an accident, but he leaned way, way over to try to keep his center of gravity as low as possible.

When the cycle began to get heavy on the right, he let the bars straighten for a few feet and let up on the rear brake a bit. The bike straightened up for about ten feet or so, and then it was back on the rear brake and the big lean to the left.

It took almost twenty seconds for the cycle to make its way down the big steep slope, and when he almost reached the bottom, he let the rear brake off and sat back up. The three-wheeled cycle straightened out and hit the flat sand at the bottom of that huge dune.

He grinned. He remembered much of his skills in dune riding from his days back on Branton. He'd been a real comer, they'd all said, in the Astillon Dune Club. He'd never been able to have his own cycle, but he had a local sponsor—a small city restaurant that was owned by an ex-rider who still loved to go out to the races. He'd offered up his bike—an older model, true, but it had been adapted and juiced up by the owner—and Tanner had been gracious to accept such generosity. In fact, he'd taken on the job of being the restaurant's dishwasher the three weekend nights, and he'd refused any paycheck. The fact that the owner really liked him made him all the more enthusiastic when it came to the dishes, taking out the garbage, bussing tables, and sorting and stacking the silverware in the server stations too.

At the same time, he'd gotten good at the Astillon Dune Club races. He'd learned the hard way that full tilt often led to learning why they make sandpaper out of sand. The number of sand burns he'd gotten at first had been so bad that twice teachers in his school had asked "So, how's things at home," and he knew they were thinking the worst. A quick two-minute vid of his latest crash coming down a dune had made them recoil with shock, but that had stopped that kind of thinking.

He waited at the bottom of the big dune and noticed the Caliph was watching from the top. He goosed his cycle and came directly down the slope but at a low speed, which was not a problem, and pulled in beside him.

He took off his helmet and tucked it in front of him onto the top of the fuel tank. He pulled off his goggles and gloves and smiled at Tanner. "That was about the best drift down a slope I've seen in thirty years. Not since my old mentor showed me how to do that and my learning how the hard way —trial and error and crash. Not so much fun—but that was masterful. Course, there is one lesson you've not learned—at least judging by today's ride," he said. And he looked at the duke.

Tanner thought for a second, as he pulled off his helmet and goggles too. "And that might be ..."

"Know the course, Tanner, before you hit the throttle—would have prevented that kind of slope being such a problem," he said.

Tanner nodded and smiled. "You got that right, Sharia—guilty as charged," he said, and that got a laugh from them both.

They'd been out on a dune ride now for almost an hour and a half. He'd come to Neria, the home planet of the Caliphate, as he'd accepted the offer to come and meet the Caliph on a more personal level. He'd not thought long about the invite, and in fact, he'd jumped at the chance. While the Caliph was an unknown, he did feel that the Caliphate itself was something to be watchful of.

He remembered some of the talks he'd had back on Halberd when as a RIM Navy captain, he'd been stationed on the prison planet and he'd met the Countess Tibah. She had spelled out the issues as the staunch supporter of Olbia—one of the planets in the Caliphate. She wanted freedom for her planet at any and all costs—and it had been Tanner, when faced with her drawing down on the man opposite him on the other cycle, who had to make the decision. He had shot and killed that assassin—no matter what his feelings were for her on a personal note. Duty above love. So the Caliph was alive because Tanner had been duty bound.

And now they sat here after a great ride today so far.

And while he was watchful of the Caliphate, the Caliph was really an unknown. Until now. Maybe.

He rubbed his left eye that had taken the occasional splash of sand. While the goggles had protected his sight, the eyebrow over there was still bearing some sand grains. He shook his head then to try to get rid of any other clinging bits, and the Caliph spoke to him.

"I asked you to come to Neria, yes, to talk about all things, but one thing that I need to mention. As you will remember, on Enki, I know that you are aware of the Xithricite and that we have been mining it in large tonnages for the years since Enki joined the Caliphate. And I know that you are aware, too, of the powers of that the Xithricite carry too." He smiled and brushed off the sand that lay on his thigh and waited.

Tanner nodded to the Caliph, knowing it was time to be totally frank. "Yes, I know that the Xithricite, when smelted and forged into panels, provides the ship clad in same with thermal invulnerability. Projectiles we know — as we tested it too, Caliph, from our few samples — still pierce the metals without a problem. Is that information that you did not know?"

The Caliph offered up half a smile and a nod. "Yes, we had our opinions on that — and it's nice to see that you're offering up the truth — the whole truth, as they say. But here is something you do not know — at least as far as we know."

He lifted a leg over the seat behind him and sat crosswise on the bike, his full race leathers in the same sandy brown colors as the landscape around him. He looked away, at the brown scene around him, as if he was making up his mind. "We," he said quietly, "have three ships totally clad in

221

Xithricite. It was so much work, you'll not know, to get the panels thick enough to be both thermally shielded and projectile shielded—up to a point. The metal plates are all within the same thickness parameters—they run at least a full ten inches of Xithricite. That's enough—at testing—to withstand all small arms fire, auto, and robo projectiles up to .50 caliber. Won't pierce the plates. Which means that these three ships are, yes, invulnerable. At least until an enemy finds a bigger caliber way to attack."

Tanner smiled. "But with space warfare swinging over to the thermal weapons, there are almost none that carry projectiles. Mines, maybe, and some have —I think it's the Novertag Navy, is it not, that has those space charges—the balls that are magnetic that seek out some steel to cling to, before drilling into the hull and exploding. But that's all that I know ..." he said.

The Caliph nodded. "True enough, those Novertag items sound like something that we might want to know more about. But we wanted you to know we've three ships—frigates actually. Older ships but with the latest technology, Tanner. And the Xithricite skins."

Tanner leaned back, hoisted a leg over the tank in front of him, and cocked his ankle over the tank itself. He studied the dunes spread out in front of them and looked all the way to the horizon.

Neria had more than sand plains and deserts, he knew, but the ruling Caliph had always lived a few miles away from where they sat, in the desert. Among the dunes and yet it had a full spaceport just a few miles away.

He looked over at the Caliph. "This news is both surprising—and at the same time, more surprising than you might think on, Sharia. I am surprised that you shared this with me—and more surprised that you were able to forge such thick panels—from an ore that is thermally invulnerable."

The Caliph clapped a hand down loudly on the tank beside him and smiled. "That we were able to forge such panels will remain a secret that the Caliphate will keep to ourselves. But that we shared it with you is not a reach. Tanner, you lead the task force on the alien intruder issue. You might need to call on us to provide some help with one or more of our red frigates in that upcoming standoff. Incidentally, the names of those new frigates have been changed to *CN Crimson I, II* and *III* ... and they are yours should they be needed."

Minutes later, they were roaring off, the Caliph gunning ahead, and Tanner thought that he'd be wise to let him lead the way. After all, it was his planet and his dunes.

#####
Tanner stood and walked to the windows. Being as angry as he was, inside the personal quarters of the Master Adept, he knew she could see his raw anger, but he didn't care. He wanted a moment to swallow this and digest it. If he could. If he wanted to swallow it—and that made him turn to her in anger. "How dare you?" he barked at her.

While she didn't flinch, she did lean back a few inches. It was good to show shame, she knew—no matter what one felt. She gathered her robe as it lay on the settee beside her, and she sent a mental tendril toward the duke.

She could see via that barest of mind links that he was surprised and mad. In fact, he was flaming mad. She just looked at him, ensuring that her face had no expression at all.

He stormed the room around the settees, walking heavily and even stomping once on some steps. "You knew. You Issians knew all about this alien intruder because they're here for you. That is something that should have been shared with the RIM Confederacy Council—or at the least with the exec committee so that we can face what we face but with a large degree of skill. More than we have."

He turned then and almost stamped his foot on the thick carpets. Unfortunately, such flooring didn't allow him to punctuate his anger with his boot soles. Here in the Master Adept's private quarters, he'd been greeted just an hour ago.

He'd been led to the Master Adept's study and had watched the Praix video first. He'd commented that the race was odd looking but that was what all non-avian races thought of those that could fly. He did think that the color of their eyes was odd, but as he had blue eyes, maybe a Praix who had orange ones was thinking the same thing.

He had then sat for almost forty more minutes as the Master Adept explained the relationship between the Praix and the Issians and that their reason for the intruder ship was to once again enslave the Issians as their own slave keepers. The Praix had groomed them for their mind reading abilities over millennia. The Praix had decided that after twenty thousand years they once again wanted the Issians back.

He had risen from his seat right in the small private study and had spewed out his anger. "You have been hiding a secret that is more than a racial or realm secret—this will affect the whole RIM Confederacy—maybe even the galaxy itself ..." he said as he sat.

He rose again and began pacing. "And then there's the wreck. You know it's what these 'Praix' aliens may want too. And that has been, what, almost two years, and you've kept the Barony in the

dark. But you knew ..." he said as he walked past
her again and then stopped and returned to sit
opposite her yet again. But he was upset and
jumped up one more time—then sat again.

He looked at her, a nursery rhyme rolling over
and over in his brain.

"We—Issians and yourself, Duke—have had
excellent relations over the past decade and more.
Much of your success here in the RIM Confederacy
can be traced back to our relationship. And we want
to continue that frankness—but you should realize
something too. That what I have just revealed to
you is a secret that is known by less than a couple of
dozen Issians. And I'm including in all of the Eons
citizens too ... millions and millions of them do not
know what you just learned. That we all came from
another galaxy, twenty-plus millennia ago. That we
were the subservient race that was in charge of the
Praix slaves—we helped keep them in line, as we
were a non-avian race, who had the power of
speech—two things the Praix do not have."

She looked down at her chest to the Issian
medallion on it and then back up at him. "And now,
yes—they're back and they want us back. They did
a mind message to us weeks ago, and they are
awaiting our answer. Why I do not know. For how
long they will sit off Ghayth, again, I do not know.
But what I do know is this—another surprise.

Those of us Issians who govern our faith—and the Eons citizens too—have made a decision. We will not go back to being the Praix slave keepers. Not now and not ever. That news, we know, will perhaps cause them to react. And we wanted you to know that above all. And yes, I will keep you in the loop, as they say. When I hear anything, you will know it within minutes."

Tanner sat still. Yes, it was news that the Issians intended to reject the Praix as their leaders once again. Yes, it was news that the Praix would find that disturbing. And it was news that, yes, he now knew and could use to make plans.

His head was spinning as he quit the rote rhyme, and he opened up his mind should the Master Adept want to see what he was thinking.

He looked at her. "Then, at least in this case, forewarned is forearmed ... but, yes, I will need to know anything else as soon as I can." His head tilted to one side for a second. "What can you tell me about the wreck itself—is there anything there that might help us? Say to use the technology we can find on the wreck against the intruder ship?"

She looked away for a second and then back at him, her hands calmly clasped in her lap. "Not at this point. I can tell you that the Baroness has sent that Roma captain—Daika, do you remember her—to look over the wreck. At this point, it appears she's not found out anything, but that could change in a moment. When I know—you'll know," she finished off, and then a small smile crossed his face...

CHAPTER EIGHT

Alver led the way down the long pathway—
walkway number one they all called it—toward the
wrecked ship's bridge. Behind him, the Roma
captain looked around in wonder. Her name was
Daika though he'd never used her first name. He
thought she was cute and very athletic looking.
*Wonder what she could do the marine obstacle test in
time-wise. Not as good as a man,* he thought, and then
he remembered Sergeant Kelly Haliburton, who'd
done the course a full twenty-seven seconds faster
than any of the male marines here in Tent City.

He grunted and continued to walk. Every so
often, the captain would ask about side pathways
and what the xeno team had found down same.

"Mostly more ship cubicles, rooms, and in one
case about half the xeno folks had an idea that that

one led to a sickbay type of space. Hanging from
the ceiling normally, but now lying on the floor,
were large metal barred cages—open on one side,
and the perches had both wires and tubes leading
out from same. Beedles had hypothesized that an
alien could simply fly into the cage while sickbay
staff would hook them up to those tubes or wires—
and in that way, the alien could be treated."

Alver had no idea if that was true or not, and he
was sure the rest of the xeno team didn't either, but
that was not his job here on the wreck site. He was
to, as of this morning, Commander Williams had
told him, accompany the captain anywhere she
wanted to go. On the wreck. Off the wreck. If she
wanted to go skinny-dipping, that too, the
commander had said dryly—and these orders came
directly to him from the Baroness and not Admiral
Vennamo.

Alver had pondered that but not enough to figure
out the real reason the captain was looking around.
He was just the tour guide, and today, that was
fine.

When they reached the bridge entryway, Alver
held out his hand. "The controls to gain entry to the
bridge we had propped open—but the recent big
change in that happened when that hum happened
and the ship 'powered up' we were told by the xeno
team. That closed the pocket bridge door—it simply

snapped right through the wooden brace we were using. Now, the only way in is to pretend to be alien, Ma'am," he said a bit sheepishly as he nodded to the two marines waiting for them.

One went up the ladder quickly to touch the circle carved into the coving about eleven feet from the floor. He then stuck a bare foot down to touch the other marine who had popped off his shirt to accept the skin-to-skin contact. The lower marine then placed his own foot carefully into the filled circle on the floor, and as soon as he did, there was a puff of air as the bridge door slid open quickly.

Motioning the captain inside, Alver nodded to his two marines and said, "Well done, lads."

The captain half-turned to see what would happen, and as she did so, the door slid closed once again.

Alver nodded. "Any entrant to the bridge has all of ten seconds to go through the opening before the door slides shut. Oh, and I've also included in the docs, for your perusal, all of the info that the xeno team has assembled on the ship itself—as well as the collateral information from the two alien warehouses we've found here too. Three maybe, but that third one is still an ongoing mystery, Ma'am."

He didn't stand at attention, but he did maintain a position slightly off the captain's hip and to her left as she walked the bridge.

With a small degree of wonder in her voice, she said, "They could run and manage a ship this large from only three console positions—am I missing something?"

Alver nodded. "Yes, Ma'am, just these three. Since the power-up of a few days ago, all the screens are now up and live and showing, I'd suspect, what they 'see,' Ma'am. One, of course," he said as he pointed, "shows only the blackness of space and galaxies in a grouping off to the right. We're still trying to find out where that view might be coming from, Ma'am," he said.

The blackness was very black, and yes, the galaxies off to the right of the screen's center were few. Five, he counted, but some of his younger lieutenants said they could discern six. *Kids*, he thought, *great eyes but can't see what's in front of them often enough.*

She nodded to him. "And that is?" she asked, pointing at a screen that showed a rock cavern, jammed with what looked like fortifications, equipment, dollies, and stacks of something on skids—the kind of items one would find at a landing port on a planet. The view, they both noted, was not changing—there was no live action. Just those items and windows of glass separating out some rooms on the one side of the huge floor.

"We know that one, Ma'am. Just discovered a few weeks back—we think it's a brand new warehouse that we only found after drone audits of that tip of a southern continent. We notified the commander as well as the admiral, Ma'am. But as yet, we've not sent a team down there. But, that screen is up and live, we think ..."

Probably correct, he thought. He'd been on the flight down there and had seen the spot with his own eyes.

Daika looked around at more. She went to the first console and tried sitting on the perch—but that put her head too far below the console monitor to see anything. She then balanced on the perch with her feet and that got her still low, but she could see the monitor's screen at least. She looked. She touched not a single button below the monitor nor the screen itself, but she asked, "Is the screen enabled, Major?" to which she got a positive nod back.

She looked. She gazed all around the large screen, and then she jumped back off the perch to look behind the screen as well. No wires. No cables. Not a single thing connected the monitor with the ship.

Alver was about to say it, but she did that for them both. "Some kind of wireless connection, I'd assume?" she said, and he nodded his assent.

She went to all three of the consoles and did the same thing. The console that was set back, alone and slightly higher than the two that sat side by side between it and the huge view-screen, the xeno team had figured was the alien captain's console. That must have occurred to her, Alver noted, as she went back and forth between all the consoles, noting which icons were lit up on each. She tapped her left shoulder, and a flash happened, and it was obvious she was taking photos of the three screens. She returned at last to lean her hip on the captain's console perch.

"Major, this is all interesting. But what do you think these aliens are all about?"

He heard her question, but he knew this was not a question for a soldier. "Ma'am, the xeno team will be able to answer that kind of query much better than I can," he said plainly.

She nodded and clapped her hands together with a solid slap. "Then let's get them here—all of them please, Major?"

He nodded, half-turned away, and then turned back. "'Ma'am, I need to leave the ship to find them to get them here. Since the 'big hum,' as we call it, our own comms do not work within the ship. Will you be okay here, or should I have the marines just outside in the bridge entryway come in to stay with you?" With no way of knowing how she'd accept that question, he hoped she'd just see that he was offering her two armed guards just in case. Of course, that led to the "in case of what" question, and he had no idea what the answer was.

She shook her head. "Not necessary, Major. I'll be fine. Tell them they won't need tablets or the like, I just want to chat," she said.

He nodded and spun, and as he walked to the door, the lights in the bridge flashed for a second or two a bit brighter, and the pocket door slid open. He went straight through, and it closed moments later.

She sighed, got off the captain's console perch, went over to the wall, and opened up a cabinet that was there.

As she noted a large shielded cable coming out of the floor inside, she grunted. About halfway up the inside of the cabinet, the cable was plugged right into a socket. This cabinet was powered. The lights on the bridge were easily now bright enough to show that. There were some flashing blue and green lights from what might have been circuit boards on the one wall of the now powered cabinet. She took a photo and closed the cabinet.

She went to each of the next twenty-six cabinets, which all stood in a row on the exterior bulkhead bridge wall. Each was opened, and Daika noted each had a power cable that was now plugged in, and she took photos at each cabinet.

She returned to sit once again, if uncomfortably at least, and looked up at the main view-screen. As the ship had plowed into the grounds here on the watery shore, the bridge was buried into the Ghayth soil so all that could be seen was blackish dirt and a rock a bit to one side. Beside it to starboard, the screen showed that as yet unexplored new warehouse, and the one to the port side showed the deep space and galaxies view.

She sat to contemplate what she knew and what she had learned from her visit so far. After reading all the notes, reports, and details of the xeno team that were in the Barony database, she did know one thing.

The "big hum," as the marines called it, was indeed responsible for turning on the ship. In all twenty-seven cabinets along the wall, the power cables had been plugged in. She did wonder how a ship's AI could do that, but as she well knew from all her years out in space, aliens do things their way. Sometimes, so surprisingly different that it was not possible to even countenance such AI capabilities. And on each of the three screens, the icon in the top right-hand corner was no longer flashing. It was on and amber in color.

Power. The wreck was powered. She knew that, and the Baroness would know too.

#####

On the *Sword*, Tanner sat in the tiny meeting room with Bram and Admiral Higgins. Before heading to Ghayth for a recon mission and trying to stay low-key, he had asked these two—his best advisers—to accompany him.

They had left Neen only a half hour ago and had used the Barony Drive to get to Ghayth in seconds. They had checked in with the Ghayth space station, the *Wilson*, just a few minutes ago.

Lieutenant Cooper had notified them that the *Sword* carried the duke and some crew—and it was their intent to just look at the alien intruder ship that hung above Ghayth.

The *Wilson* replied and made the request that the *Sword* stay at least twice as far away from the alien ship as their force fields reached out—about twenty miles or so was judged safe—and the lieutenant had acknowledged same.

They sat about a hundred miles off and watched the enormous alien ship just sitting there in orbit, doing nothing. The usual ultra-bright teal ray reached out from within the alien ship's force field, centered on the *Sword* for a second or two, and then winked out.

"They see us," Cooper had said. "That's how they find out who's around—or so they tell me."

More than a mile long, it's upper and lower tubed areas maintained their position in space while the huge central disk was slowly rotating around that axis. That central round disk was about seven or eight hundred feet tall and jutted out at least a half mile from the ship's axis. There looked like some landing bays, and one disappeared as the disk rotated and another came into view. There were also portholes—hundreds of them—lit from within too.

Like everyone else, Tanner tried to figure out what the different things on the ship were. The disk rotated and what Tanner believed was the top came into view. On the top of that disk were arrays and pods that one might guess could be this or that, but all the humans truly had no idea at all.

"Using human standards to figure out what something is for is always a lesson in futility," Bram said, and the three of them nodded as they watched the view-screen in their meeting room.

Admiral Higgins began. "Duke, we need—well, sorry, Your Grace, we think that we would like to —"

"Don't pussyfoot around me, Admiral—you have more experience than I do in this kind of situation," Tanner said.

The admiral nodded. "Sir—we would like to come up with a plan—rules of engagement for this encounter. It's a first contact for sure—and at this point, one that is still up in the air. We've no idea if it will turn to be adversarial—but like all admirals who may have to send navy ships into battle, we want as much on our side as we can muster, Your Grace."

He tapped a finger on the table and went on. "We need to consider this—that in their minds, we may be just vermin here. That they will, when it suits them, just take out every RIM realm ship the same way that they took out that Novertag drone ship." His voice was firm. He'd been here before, and he wanted enough cards in his hand to win the pot.

Tanner held up a hand to stop his admiral. He had decided how far he could spread out information, and these two were surely a part of winning. It took almost a full thirty minutes for him to bring the two of them up to speed.

He talked first of the red metal ships—Xithricite-encased frigates—from the Caliphate. Both of them had known about the red metal, and both had also had high enough rank to have seen the lab reports about the metal back when they were all Barony Navy men. The lab reports had shown the Xithricite was impervious to any thermal attack but susceptible to projectiles. The Caliph had used ten-inch thick plates on the frigates, and they'd survive up to a full .50-caliber projectile.

The admiral looked excited at that piece of news, and he pointed over at the alien ship. "And from what we can see—reports from the *Wilson* argue the same—their ship appears to not have any weapons arrays, and there's not a single piece of evidence that they have any projectile weapons either. Good news that is, Sir!" he said and slapped the table.

"That's the good news," Tanner said, "and now here's the bad ..."

He then went on to explain to them that the Praix had appeared here in the RIM Confederacy to get their Issian slave masters back in the fold. It was complicated, but he did try to explain as much as the Master Adept had given him, in respect to reconnaissance.

"The Praix, the owners of the alien ship just sitting there, had been on Ghayth twenty-thousand years ago. They had been looking into colonizing the Milky Way, and the Issians were a part of their crew. The colonization plans had gone astray, and there'd even been a huge crash down onto Ghayth, which the Baroness was trying to find technology from.

"When the Praix had arrived those weeks ago, we all thought they did nothing but sit out there. Not true. They sent a message to the Master Adept via some kind of mind link that had included the twelve members of the Issian inner circle.

According to this message, the Praix wanted the Issians back. They needed the Issians to start to conquer this new—to them—galaxy, beginning here on the RIM.

"The Master Adept shared with me that the Issians had all agreed—they wanted no part in this. Their independence was all that any Issian would countenance. She confirmed that the wreck below and the warehouses found, located, and now in study were, yes, all Praix owned.

Bram had tried to interrupt three times, and each time, Tanner had stopped him, but now he bared his arm, sliding up a sleeve, and offered it to Bram. Bram nodded and gripped the duke's arm—linking their minds. A minute later, Bram nodded and let go.

"Bram, as you can see, I believed the Master Adept when she told me that the Issian race would rather die—than go back to being the Praix slave masters. Now you've seen what I saw ..."

Bram agreed and looked at his duke. "Your Grace—yes, I do see that. But where does that leave us? If these Praix want Issians, and they—we—say no, will that not lead to a war?"

The admiral jumped in. "What we need to do is to get those three ships here ASAP. Put good captains in charge. Your Grace, you should not be a part of that force. Instead, sit here on the *Sword* so

241

that you can oversee the action—when and if there is some, Sir," he said.

Tanner looked out at the slowly rotating alien ship, sighed, and nodded. "Same advice I got this morning from the wife," he said, and that got a couple of chuckles from them.

Tanner leaned forward. "Oh, and I would also add this strange fact—the Master Adept said that I was 'destined' for this. That so much here on the RIM has been with me at the focus that this too would be something that I was supposed to be a part of too." He sighed once more, noting that the admiral had a look on his face of dawning knowledge.

"Your Grace, that does begin to resonate with me … after all, wasn't it you who—"

Tanner held up his hand and nodded in agreement. "Yes, and I've no idea why that has happened nor for that matter whether or not it will again lead to success in the future," he said.

Bram smiled. "Your Grace … like an old instructor of mine used to say back at the Eons Naval Academy—why worry when you've still aces to play …"

Now all three of them smiled and turned once again to look out on the Praix ship, still in orbit and still waiting …

#####

"Engineering flock leader—any changes in the past few days?" the Praix captain asked right out loud, as he jumped up on his captain's perch and touched the screen in the top left corner.

While the ship's AI would, of course, recognize that someone—a Praix—was now seated at the captain's console, only touching the corner of the screen let the AI validate that Praix as the true captain. The touch meant that an instant DNA test had been done, and yes, the captain was in his chair.

It was a holdover from thousands of years in their past, when the first basic AI routines had been written to validate the entry of a Praix in a nest. Was this the nest that this particular Praix should have entry to was the sum of that routine, and even now, the same routines were being used.

The engineering flock leader, sitting to the right-hand side and in front of the captain, swiveled on its perch and looked at the captain. Pointing at the display in front of it as it shifted its feet on its perch, its beak snapped as it sent the answer to the captain with a mental push.

"No changes since yesterday, when a single new ship arrived. Small, what we'd call a shuttle in size, we beamed it, of course, and it had only four occupants. They stayed about two hours—and then left. Which

leaves what appears to be the same four—the space station and three warships just sitting and watching us."

The captain clacked his beak to say good, and then he looked over at the other console on the bridge and sent through a message to that Praix bridge officer. *"Any word from the Issians? We have been waiting now almost long enough. Send the message once more to their Master Adept and remind her that it is our last attempt. After, say, another three days, we will take it that their silence means a no—and we will proceed with that answer in mind."*

He shook his right wing and flexed the feathers along the middle coverts of that wing, stretching the tendons below and easing a bit of a cramp. These Issians, according to what he'd originally read in the Praix database, should have jumped at the opportunity after twenty millennia of being without the Praix to serve. They had been marooned here in this galaxy that was empty of the Praix masters, and that too should have meant they wanted back into the flock.

The Praix intended to own the RIM first, and then from there, the rest of the galaxy would be theirs ...

Tanner sat in the navy administration building, having borrowed a room from the admiral. The admiral had wanted Tanner to use his office, but Tanner had nicely turned down that offer—and had accepted a meeting room down the hall. He'd asked for a small pot of tea—any kind—and had gratefully accepted the steaming green tea and had poured his own, shooing out the navy steward.

Tanner sat and drank his tea slowly, savoring the cup with only a touch of milk this time. Usually he added lemon but not this time. He sipped and thought. And then he knew that he had to make the EYES ONLY call and ask for help.

While he didn't know what kind of help the Baroness might hold for him, he did know that the RIM task force was only partially ready to defend the RIM Confederacy at this point. The next sip of tea took a bit, as he nursed it and then nodded to himself. *Time*, he thought.

He leaned over to the console, hit the right sequence of buttons, placed his palm on the security panel, and was recognized as the Duke d'Avigdor. He hit a couple more buttons, and the screen in front of him was black at first followed by the twin crowns in red and blue on a shield, the icon of the Barony of Neres.

A few moments later, the icon disappeared, and the smiling face of the Baroness appeared.

He dipped his head and said, "Welcome, Baroness, so nice that you were able to talk to me this afternoon," he said, with a high degree of respect in his voice. He too was a Royal now, but a major part of being a Royal was following tradition and protocol.

She smiled at him, and then from beside her, a hand holding a tall glass of white wine appeared, and she accepted it with a wave and a thank you. She took a quick sip and then placed the glass down on the table in front of her. And then she nodded at him. "How nice to see you again, Duke d'Avigdor. What might I ask is the call about today?"

He smiled back at her and began to explain to her what the task force was currently about when it came to the alien intruder ship.

He pointed out what he'd learned from the Issians first. That the aliens—the Praix they were called—were here on the RIM to get the Issians to come back into their society as slave masters. The Praix intended to first conquer the RIM Confederacy, planet by planet. It would be the Issians' job to get total obedience from the realms, one by one, and make them obey the Praix.

She looked shocked, as she swallowed that. "Are you ... well ... sure about that, Duke? I mean that is so beyond the pale—"

And he interrupted her. *A duke can do that, at least I hope so.* "Ma'am, yes, this comes directly from the

Master Adept. I have been granted access to the Issian history of how twenty or so thousand years ago, they were left on Eons by the Praix after their disastrous attempt at establishing an outpost on Ghayth. Yes, the wreck is their own. So are the contents of the warehouses that have been found too—all three of them, Ma'am."

She nodded.

He went on to talk about the Caliph next. "On their way to Neen are three new frigates that are clad in Xithricite, ten inches thick, and those frigates should be able to help in any battle with the Praix. The Caliph has offered them to the task force with not a thing in return." Twice, Tanner stressed that the Caliph did not ask for anything in return and tried to show that fact alone was important. "For better relations within the RIM Confederacy, Ma'am," he added, and in response, the Baroness nodded.

He did mean that too. It augured well for the RIM Confederacy. That was something he'd believe and work with no matter whether the red ships helped in battle or fell to the Praix.

She picked up her glass of wine and stared at him as she took a drink and then another, and finally tilting the glass back, she drained it completely.

She looked away for a moment and then back at him, and before he could continue, she held up a hand to stop him. "Duke. In that same spirit, let me make the following offer. We, too, have been mining our own Xithricite from a location down in Pentyaan space. Surreptitiously, of course, but we have been able to acquire more than four tons of same. It's been smelted and forged into hull panels, and we have a large shuttle—two hundred feet in length—now suitably clad. The panels that we used are a full foot thick, as we too wanted to avoid any projectile damage as well as the Caliph. We now offer our shuttle too, named the *Defiant*, crewed by Barony Navy officers, of course, but under the leadership of you—the task force leader."

She nodded and another glass of wine appeared in moments. Now that the hard part was out of the way, Tanner noticed she was this time dressed in shades of red. Bright and dull, rusty and shiny, smooth and rough—but the colors all shimmered as she sat and moved even slightly in front of her monitor.

He smiled at her. "Baroness, I had no idea, of course—but I do thank you for your openness and the offer as well. Have the ship come over to Neen immediately as we'll be launching our ships in just a few days. I thank you for that, gratefully, Ma'am," he said as he dipped his head toward her.

She leaned forward and reached for the new glass of wine. "I also sent the Roma captain—Daika

Rossum, I think you might remember—to Ghayth too. I thought that she could maybe look at the wreck and see it with different eyes. The eyes of a scavenger who sees things that maybe our xeno team has overlooked in the past year or so. All that she found—and perhaps she puts more importance on this than I do—was that in her opinion, the wreck—the Praix I guess—their AI is very much superior to what we have and expect. She put great stock in this, but how one can use that to defeat them, I have no idea. Perhaps you will?" She sipped her wine and just stared at him.

He nodded and his answer was simple. "We have no idea, but it's good to know in case," he said as he shrugged.

She nodded.

He nodded back, and they signed off. As he did, he thought that had been a good call and having the Baroness respond to the unspoken challenge of matching the Caliph's offer had worked. Of course, he had had no idea that it might get him another Xithricite-clad ship.

He smiled. *Now hopefully with that good news too, I might be able to sleep tonight ...*

CHAPTER NINE

Off Ghayth, near the *Wilson*, the planet's space station, the ensemble cast of ships was staid. The *Wilson* was on one side of the ship, and then at three points around the Praix intruder ship lay the frigate the *RN Coventry* and two cruisers, the *RN Whitney* and the *RN Newton*. The feelings were that with the intruder ship surrounded, so to speak, that anything changing that formation would be instantly seen by the RIM forces.

Just a half hour ago, the *Sword* had dropped out of subspace and now sat between the *Wilson* and the *Coventry*. As usual, she'd been subjected to that ultra-bright teal ray that instantly popped out of the intruder ship whenever a new ship appeared. It read the *Sword* as a vessel, they all thought, and Tanner did so too, and then the ray snapped off.

"They know we're here," he said to no one in
particular on the *Sword* bridge area and heads did
nod.

"Give us a tour, please, Lieutenant," Tanner said
to his pilot.

Cooper acknowledged the request with "Aye,
Your Grace," and the *Sword* swung around to go
around the Praix ship.

Big, Tanner thought, *very, very big.* The *Atlas* was
the biggest ship on the RIM at almost eighteen
hundred feet, but preliminary measurements
showed the Praix ship was more than three
thousand feet longer. How it ran was an unknown.
How many Praix were aboard was an unknown.
How they'd take to the refusal by the Issians was an
unknown.

Tanner called for a halt when the *Sword* made the
last corner around the Praix ship and again took its
position beside the *Wilson.*

There were many unknowns, but one thing was
for sure—as the Praix ship sat here, it was a threat
that was unstated as yet. *That was what the task force,
under his command, was concerned with,* he thought as
he had another sip of the too hot tea and sucked in
some air to try to cool his tongue. He put the tea
mug down and looked over at Bram. "Here goes—
and this may not be the answer that we're looking
for—but worth the try," he said. He nodded to

Cooper. "Send the call, Lieutenant."

Cooper said, "Aye, Your Grace" and made some keyboard commands.

Ten minutes later, off to port, the *Crimson I*, the red metal Caliphate ship with its ten-inch-thick hull plates of Xithricite, popped in. It was about a mile off from the Praix ship, slowly moving on impulse power to sit nearer the *Wilson*.

Tanner's breath was held, and as he watched, he stared at the *Crimson I*. He waited a moment and then sucked in a big breath of air. A full minute had passed since the Caliphate ship had popped into existence.

No ultra-bright teal ray.

None of the usual monitoring of the ships around the Praix ship had taken place.

The Praix, therefore, could not "see" the *Crimson I* — the Xithricite hid the ship's existence. Tanner smiled and let out a big sigh.

"Looks like the red metal keeps that ship undetectable," Bram said. With an ear-to-ear grin, he hollered, "Woo-hoo!"

Even the pilot, Lieutenant Cooper grinned back at him, and Tanner nodded to him and said, "Bring in the other two."

Cooper turned back to complete that order.

Twenty minutes later, the red metal Caliphate ships were in position around the Praix intruder ship.

The *Crimson II* sat off the port side of the *Whitney*. *Crimson III* sat off the port side of the *Newton*, and the first in, the *Crimson I*, sat just to the left of the *Coventry*. Each of the Caliphate ships was positioned around the alien ship, and each was partnered with a RIM Navy ship at the same time.

The *Sword's* Ansible station lit up, and during the next half hour or so, the discussions between the six captains of the ships—the three Caliphate Navy ships and the three RIM Navy ships—were all involved in the strategy of their mission. Each agreed that the three Caliphate ships had not been detected by the intruder ship. Each captain felt that was because of the Xithricite hull plating as that was the only difference. The Caliphate ships were frigates, each six hundred feet long, and the same size as the *Coventry*—so there could be no other answer.

Six ships now circled the intruder ship—and only three could be seen by the aliens. The discussions ended and Tanner signed off on the task force captains' Ansible conference call.

While Tanner knew it was a good thing the aliens couldn't see all the ships, it wasn't a real answer. That would come when the Praix learned they were not going to be successful in reacquiring the Issians as their slave masters. Time would tell was the old adage that came to mind, and he sipped from his tea that had finally cooled down.

#####

After a quick jump back to Neen, Tanner had the *Sword* land on the Duchy d'Avigdor landing port. He was walking off the ramp when Lieutenant Cooper flagged him down from behind. He stood in the access port itself and called out to his duke.

"Your Grace, Major Stal is calling for you — should I transfer the Ansible over to your PDA?" he asked.

Tanner responded, "Yes, please," and as he walked, the PDA on his left wrist vibrated once. He grinned as he hit the receive button, and a hologram of Alver appeared above his wrist

"Your Grace — so good of you to take this call," Stal said, a big grin on his face.

"And nice for you to call me — what's up, Major?" he replied.

Alver looked down at a tablet and then back up at the duke with a grin. "It appears that the Baroness is sending along, from Neres, a shuttle to join the task force, I've just been told. It will be under command of one Captain Magnusson — you know him, I believe?" he said.

Tanner nodded. Yes, the captain had been a Barony Navy man, and he'd had some dealings with him before. He'd been the "loose cannon" who'd used the just released Barony Drive to jump to Branton—Tanner's home world—some thirteen hundred lights inward on his shakeout cruise. That alone was odd enough, but the captain had been under his eye often before when he'd been the Barony admiral.

"Yes, I know him," he responded.

"And I'm to gather two platoons of my best marines and board the shuttle—she's named the *Defiant*, I understand. Will be cramped for us—but marines adapt," Alver said, the smile still plastered on his face.

Tanner nodded and signed off after sending word to the *Wilson* that they were to send down a shuttle to Ghayth to pick up the marines and hold them. Also, they were to Ansible to the *Defiant* to pick up their marines from the *Wilson*. He also sent another message to the task force captains; they were to watch and record the entry of the *Defiant* as it popped into space in their vicinity for any sign of whether the ultra-bright teal ray had been used or not..

As he walked into the administration building, he took the escalator down to the secure area, passed through some of the bonded cargo areas and the brig, and went right to the end of the long hallway.

There, he placed his hand on the access plate and allowed the retina scan to look into his eyes, and he grinned at the camera at the same time.

Going through the doors, he nodded to some of the folks in lab coats he met, and a minute later, he was in the lab where he found the man he was looking for, CWO Hartford. He smiled at the Tarvos native, sat on a stool at the lab counter, and waited.

Hartford waved at him as he finished some kind of a notation on a glass beaker, writing with a grease pencil on the side of same, and then came over. He asked for the room, and the two others inside left them alone.

Tanner said, "You messaged me with news that you'd made a breakthrough, Chief?" he asked, his one foot on the floor as he leaned on the edge of the table.

Hartford nodded, got up, and went over to a bench on the wall. He took up one of the belts, brought it back, and laid it on the table in front of him. He sat once again on a stool a few feet apart from Tanner.

"Your Grace, yes, we have made some progress— at least from what we had originally had, knowledge-wise, about these power belts," he began as he picked one up and held it between them.

"Composition—we don't know this element, but it is an alloy between the unknown metal and steel.

That we do know. We have searched Gallipedia as well as every single engineering, metallurgy, and science database we know—and the metal is an unknown element. So much of a mystery as we can't even find out its structure, molecular, and rhombohedral crystal layouts either. We will continue to work on this, but at this point, we're stumped," he said.

Tanner thought his voice held frustration more than anything else, and he knew that once a Tarvos citizen got his teeth into something, it would be worked on until an answer was found.

Hartford continued, his voice a bit apologetic. "Time of manufacture was, or rather is, still a difficult one. We cannot find any way to date when these power belts were made. By whom. Where they were made. How they were made. Why they were made might be easier, but it surely was for a defensive reason. We're stumped there, Your Grace."

Hartford leaned a bit closer, his hands with the two thumbs holding the belt intertwined with his fingers. "But what we did learn was accidental—I must say that right up front, Your Grace. While we were studying the power belt, as it was in testing, we tried every single item we could to get it to fail. Not a single thing we tried—energy pulse cannons, lasers, plasma cannons, a Merkel, a Colt, a needler, a stun gun—was successful. All failed to pierce the protective shield. Which is what we knew, of course," he said as he placed the belt on the table beside them, paused, and looked at Tanner.

Tanner nodded and gestured for Hartford to continue.

"And yes, testing from within the belt itself—that is, a wearer of the power belt when it was turned on was unable to shoot any gun, carbine, or rifle that would go through the power belt shield at an attacker. Nor would a laser, and even one of those large handheld mobile energy pulse weapons. Being inside the power belt shield meant that there was a wall between the wearer and reality. At least that was our thinking. So, we were stumped."

He shifted in his seat a bit, and Tanner noticed that his ears—big Tarvos ears—were suddenly blushing. "And I must apologize, Your Grace, for what happened next, though it did lead to a discovery. One of my senior lab assistants had failed once again in his attempts to get any kind of weapon to work as he wore the belt and shot at the targets," he said. He pointed over to a glass-walled area that was their practice testing range as if to emphasize the next thing he was going to say.

"He turned the belt off and threw it with some force down at the floor. Our solid steel decking, and the power belt buckle, broke open. I say broke, but maybe a better word is was forced open?" He shook his head, his large ears almost flapping, and he wiped his chin with a thumb, the rest of that hand closed up in a fist.

"The buckle broke open?" Tanner questioned.

"It did. We immediately looked inside, and yes, there is some kind of a circuit board there—an Ansible board from further testing, we were able to determine. Ansible science, we know, and that includes in the frequency of the various factors that create the subspace immediate real-time communications. Frequency comes from the Ansible crystals within the circuit board, and it was the first thing we found of interest. While there may be others, the thing is, Your Grace, we can control, at least at this point, in a limited fashion, the power belt's shielding," he said.

Tanner wondered for a second if he should address the hissy fit the lab assistant had had, and then he realized that kind of micromanaging was way beneath a duke's pay grade. Instead, he said, "Can I see, Chief?"

And that got a real smile from Hartford, who said right away, "Of course, Your Grace—let me call my assistants back in."

In moments, Tanner and the chief stood in front of the glass separating the lab from the practice range. The chief pushed the talk button on the wall in front of them. "Okay, Alex, carry the target, and please make an adjustment on the buckle to allow you to shoot from within the power belt—and Bill, stand off to one side with the laser," he said.

Alex, one of the assistants wearing a white lab coat, reached down and into the buckle's innards and made some kind of a modification. He put the belt on and then picked up a handheld target with one hand and a small handheld laser with the other. Using his index finger, he turned the belt on. Standing ten feet away from him, the other lab assistant, Bill, also picked up a small laser with one hand and a target with his other hand. Then they waited for the good to go from the chief.

Hartford looked at the duke, got a nod, and then said, "Go" into the wall mic.

On the other side of the wall, the testing began. Bill pointed the laser toward Alex who wore the belt, and he aimed directly at the target held outstretched by Alex to one side. The laser was getting through the shield as the target was beginning to smoke even though these were low-level lasers and at their lower settings.

"As you can see, the setting that Alex made on the buckle now allows a laser to get by the shield," the chief said as he nodded to Alex.

Alex turned on his laser and aimed at the target that Bill held. The laser beam came right out of the power belt shield, and Bill's target began to smoke too.

The chief said, "As you can see, an adjustment in the Ansible crystals means that the lasers are no longer being stopped by the power belts. Everything else still is not allowed to enter or leave. So our testing has shown that we cannot segregate the direction of what can pierce the power belt shields but only control the weapon granted access itself," he said as the two assistants cleaned up the range and left them alone once more.

Seated back on his stool, Tanner asked the question that had come to mind right off the bat. "So, if we know what weapons a foe has—we can protect a belt wearer from same—do I have that right?"

"Exactly, Your Grace. Foreknowledge will be a huge advantage," he answered.

"Projectiles—can the Ansible be set to allow, say, a bullet but not a thrown rock?" He had searched for a polarized point.

"Yes, from what we can tell, there are more than —at a rough count only, Your Grace—hundreds of frequencies. We've tested only the first dozen or so, since this 'accidental' breakthrough of yesterday."

"Would the changes that you make be a user allowed item, Chief ... or is this done at the factory level only?"

The chief shrugged. "I do not know, Your Grace. We still have no method of inserting any kind of a tool or fingernail even to get the buckles to open. A study of the practice testing range vids showed us the exact spot to hit with the right amount of force, and we can reproduce that on all of the belts we have to get the buckles open. Further study is necessary, Your Grace," he said and smiled.

Tanner grinned back. "You are so charged with that duty now, Chief. But if you can 'jury-rig' some kind of a jig for us to use to simply place a belt inside and, say, press down on a lid of some kind that will pop open the belt buckles—that will help. We've a need for about thirty or so belts to all be modified. Can that be done ASAP?" he asked.

The chief's head was tilted to one side as he thought, and then he grinned back at Tanner. "Yes, I think we can rig something up by end of today, Your Grace. Just send us the belts and the weapon lists of what you want to allow 'in' and 'out,' and we can do all that by end of tomorrow."

On the way back to the *Sword*, Tanner was busy on his PDA.

One EYES ONLY message was sent to the Leudie Trade Master Lofton for thirty new belts and cautious low-key news that the quest for a belt that would allow the wearer to wield a weapon had succeeded. The belts, he had said, were needed today. Now.

Major Stal, on Ghayth, was the next one to receive an EYES ONLY message. Tanner told him that he wanted a quick recon down on the wreck to see if there was any kind of weaponry that had been found—small arms, specifically—that would have been wielded by the Praix. So far, Tanner had seen not a single item in that category, but he'd been out of the Barony Navy for more than a year, so there might have been some new finds that he'd not been privy with.

The final EYES ONLY message was to his wife with the news that he was on Neen and would be home for dinner. That message made him smile; they'd not been together very much in the past few weeks. "Honeymoon's over," he said to himself, "and the life of being a Royal was a real user-up of time ..."

#####

As he strode down the major path between the rows of tents, Alver was of a mind that this mission would not bear fruit. The duke had asked him— well, the head of the RIM Confederacy task force had asked a Barony marine—for help. But in his eighteen months of duty here on Ghayth, he'd heard nothing himself about weapons on the wrecked ship.

As he got to the end of the path, where the big dining tent was pitched, he stopped for a second to look out at the huge lake to his left. He shook his head. *Huge lake, the research team says ... huh, still looks like a small sea to me,* he thought. Mushroom trees were braving the brisk winds that came from offshore, and he could see whitecaps out there too. In surprise, he realized the air was clear of the mist that normally hung over the shoreline, and he could see all the way to the horizon.

"Damn—those climate guys are good," he said to himself, and he turned to his right to enter the tent and went over to the far side to sit down with the two members of the xeno team he'd called to meet him.

Professor Reynolds, the head of the xeno team was an old hand at the kind of science that was required to dig out facts from ancient relics. Alver had looked up each of the team back when they'd first been shipped here from Neres, and this man was pretty much the poster boy for alien races and their toys.

Beside him sat Professor Beedles, the xeno team member to whom all devices—things that were meant to be picked up and held or used as tools—were sent. He had reported over the past almost two years everything he had found. He had found things as mundane as toothbrushes, which had been later updated to be beak cleaners. He had reported on the alien's ladders that so far had been left as a standing find. He had reported on more than two hundred items. And none had even been postulated as being a weapon, or so his reports had said.

Now, to get the word from the horse's mouth, Alver thought. "Gentlemen—thank you for finding time to meet with me," he said.

The two nodded but said nothing.

"I need to know—the duke has asked me to ask you both personally as to your finds on the wreck over the whole time you've been here. Did you find weapons? Handheld weapons? Of any kind of type —or even something as yet not even indexed or categorized as a weapon?" he said.

He looked at the two of them, and they did not look at each other at all. *Good sign,* he thought, as he knew people colluding often reached out for eye contact before telling the same lie.

Reynolds half-smiled at him and put down his tablet. "One thing about being on a xeno team, Major, is that you quickly realize that what you think is a delicious appetizer is merely shoe polish. We bring no knowledge about the Praix to this xeno team search. There are no printed records we can find, photos of them holding this or using that. We know only that they were this size and could fly."

Beedles added, "And used ladders. And that

their crewmembers database could be updated by simply turning one on," he added.

That stopped Alver cold. "Pardon? Could you expand on that and also how you know that the ship's database was updated too?"

Beedles preened a bit, Alver thought, as he was being asked for more information based on his own xeno team testing.

"Surely, Major. Astin and I—she's the xeno team member in technology—were working down in the cargo bay areas in what we think are the Praix tools warehousing section. She and I were testing round steel or some kind of steel alloy disks that ended up being our alien ladders.

"We decided to try to get one to work, so she took one down off the wall, as well as an amber-colored filter. Placing the filter over the steel disk meant she had to put her finger over an LED switch. At least we thought it was a switch. That gave her a shock—not a big one, mind you, she said, and it turned on the disk that now emitted an amber glow. It floated two feet off the deck. No matter what we did, including both of us getting up on it, it would not sink.

"Anti-grav for sure, and that was the big import of the testing of that device. But in hindsight, the fact that Astin was shocked, we felt, was a part of the alien database being updated, as further tests showed that she and she alone on the xeno team could get some things working," he said.

Professor Reynolds jumped in right then. "And, Major, we'd like to, once again, request that we get access back into the wreck. Something caused that big hum those days and days ago, and we'd like to see what that meant inside. Instead of getting blocked by your marines who are still refusing access.

"And no, we've found not a single instance of any device that is a weapon. Nothing that is similar to what we have—small arms or rifles or carbines— not a single thing has been found. Now, we were only about twenty percent through the ship so far ... again another reason that we now need full access— doorways that were locked may now be open," he said, a bit exasperatedly.

His voice, Alver thought, *was frustrated. Upset. Not mad but still wondering why the xeno team could not enter.*

So he nodded and clapped the professor's arm where it lay on the table. "I've asked for that same thing, Professor—and hope to hear back from the commander or even Neres soon too."

He turned to Beedles. "Please forward to me the reports—not a host of same, just the few that talk about the discovery of the ladder—and how later you found that your xeno team member had been, somehow, added to the Praix database. Today, please," he added and rose.

"Of course, Major," Beedles replied.

"I need to get up to the *Wilson* soon, gentlemen, so a quick reminder—those reports as soon as possible, and please keep this meeting and our talk confidential. I know I can count on you both," he said as he strode away.

He was lost in thought, but admittedly, he had nothing on Praix weapons to help the task force with, he knew. *Of course, how to add a human to the Praix database giving more access to shipboard systems —now that was interesting ...* he thought and strode the path leading out of the tent city and toward a shuttle that waited for him. *Got to let the duke know ASAP ...*

On the *Wilson*, Captain Magnusson was waiting with some degree of impatience. He'd brought the *Defiant* over to Ghayth and had gotten orders awaiting him that he was to dock on the station and pick up a couple of platoons of Barony marines. That wasn't the issue—the issue was that the orders directly from the duke were that the marine major was to be in charge once the ship took up its own picket duty around the Praix intruder ship.

He'd already heard about the fact that the aliens

had not used that ultra-bright teal ray to find the *Defiant*, due, he'd also learned, to the fact that it was clad in Xithricite hull plates. He thought that was a comfort until he'd looked around and had noted that there were already three frigates clad in the exact same hull plates, their redness easy to see. He had gone from being the only ship that could withstand all space weapons to now being the smallest of the four with the same degree of invulnerability.

Frustrated. And now impatient that the marines were taking so much time. He barked at a lieutenant across the landing bay deck a few feet away. "Mind telling me what the hell is taking a few dozen marines so bloody long to get down here?" he asked.

The lieutenant slid his tablet down to his side. "Sir, they're all in cargo bay number three, just one deck up, getting some armory items, I was told. I can message them to move up to double-time, Sir?" he asked, staring straight out in front of him.

Magnusson sighed. *Two platoons were about, what, eighty soldiers maybe? How long to get a new rifle or something and then show up down one deck in the landing bay?* He spun on his heel and went over to the *Defiant* and back up the landing ramp, leaving word to the duty officer posted at the bottom of the ramp to notify him as soon as the marines were aboard. He walked off to his left at first to take a side corridor to the major corridor that ran the whole length of the ship and then left again to the bridge. While shuttles normally had a very limited bridge, this one, at more than one hundred fifty feet in length, did have a ready room. At least that's what he called it—he'd been told that it used to be a storage room for extra gear in a previous life before the shuttle had been re-commissioned as the *Defiant* and outfitted with its brand new invulnerable Xithricite hull plating.

He entered the small room, and the door closed behind him. He took one of the six seats around the center table. He quickly called up the ship's AI and asked for a view from one of the picket ships of the Praix intruder ship, and in moments, he was looking out at same.

The Praix ship stood still, as normal, and around it laid the task force ships. Surrounding the Praix ship were three RIM navy ships and three Caliphate ships, their red hulls easy to see. "Not so easy for the Praix though," he said to himself.

Course, he rationalized, *so what? Didn't matter that the ships couldn't be seen, their weapons would undoubtedly fail to enter the intruder ship force field like all other ships. Right,* he thought.

He nodded. That did make sense.

He watched nothing happen for another full half

hour and a bit, and then there was a knock at the
ready room door.

He grunted and yet said, "Come in."

Major Stal entered and snapped off a salute to the
captain of the *Defiant*. "Major Stal, reporting in, Sir.
Sorry to have delayed our deployment—we only
got word about the last-minute items two hours
ago, Sir. But, both platoons on board and encamped
in cargo bay number two. Cozy, but we're fine,
Sir," he said.

Magnusson nodded and waved to one of the
seats opposite him. "Thank you, Major. Good to
have you aboard. May I ask—what kind of
armament did you just get issued?" he asked,
wondering what someone thought might be of help
against a force-field-protected alien ship.

Alver nodded and rose once more. He undid his
utility belt and then the bottom two buttons on his
camouflage shirt. From beneath that cover,
Magnusson could see a simple red linked belt.

"A belt?" he asked.

Alver nodded and then looked over at the
captain's side. "I see that you're wearing a needler,
Captain. Can I ask," he said as his hand snaked
down to find the power belt buckle and made some
kind of a movement behind the buckle, "that you
shoot me with that needler, Sir—no need to worry,
Sir, the belt is invulnerable to a needler."

This I gotta see. Magnusson thought. "Fine, Major, but do step away from the table, no sense in you hitting your head when the needler takes you down," he said. He drew and aimed the needler directly at the marine's chest and hit the trigger button.

Nothing happened at all. He grimaced, then stopped firing, and slid the power button up to full —and he hit the trigger button again.

Nothing happened. The marine was smiling at him and not falling to the deck in pain.

Magnusson turned off the needler and re-holstered it on his side. He waved the marine to sit. He stared at the belt for a moment or two and then began to ask rapid-fire questions.

Stal waited until Magnusson had asked all of his questions before he answered a single question. "Yes," the marine said, "the power belt would protect him from any type of space weapons.

"Yes, the whole two marine platoons were now wearing such belts.

"Yes, they were in fact invulnerable, but with a certain set of circumstances, they could fight back.

"Yes, the only weapon that could pierce the belt's shields was a projectile weapon."

Stal reached over to his own sidearm and held up the fully automatic pistol. "Only this kind of bullet can pierce the power belt's shield—a .454 Casull.

It's what we shoot—and what the belt will accept both outgoing and incoming. The fact that the Casull, even though it had huge knockdown power, had fallen out of manufacture more than five centuries ago helps a bit, in that we are counting on the fact that the Praix do not have such a caliber— nor for that matter any kind of projectile weapons either. At least that's the skinny," Alver said.

Magnusson sat back. He looked out at the intruder ship still floating within the ring of the task force ships and then back at the major. "Major, I hope to God that they don't have such weapons— but to count one's life on that is what I might call foolhardy," he said.

Alver nodded. "Aye, Captain, but then we're marines, aren't we?"

CHAPTER TEN

Tanner stood at the window and once again tried to yank the heavy drapes across the full width of the window. He'd not been able to see in one corner of the big view-screen in the duke's study, and he cursed the curtain rod for not giving him some slack.

From behind him, a voice called out. "I know you're getting ready for the alien confrontation— would you rather use the old duke's real 'war room' than try to modify that drapery, Tanner?" Helena stood there, looking at him as he swung around and said, "Huh, hon?"

She nodded. At least he'd partially heard her. "You do remember that I took the guided tour of our new palace, and one of the rooms, was called the ducal war room, down on the third floor—and I

274

have the location right here," she said as she held up her wrist to show him her PDA.

He grinned. "Yes, please, my dear ... lead on." He left the drapes partway open and followed her.

They headed out the door and to his right. They walked down the long residential-level main corridor to the private escalator and took it down a level. On the third floor, they walked hand in hand through the security access point that was invisible but monitored by the ducal palace AI. She took a side corridor about a hundred feet along to the right, and that took them toward the rear of the palace. At a doorway on her right, she stopped and gave him a big sweeping gesture.

"My Duke—here is your war room," she said ,and she opened the door and allowed him to go in.

"War room it is," he said to himself, as he walked in just a couple of steps. On his left were wall-to-wall, ceiling-to-floor view-screens all with various displays. Some he saw were pointed at the Neen navy yards and others at the big landing port in the capital just a few miles away. Three of the screens were just black, waiting to be told what to show. In front of him was a single seat at a semi-circular desk with a whole row of parallel monitors, all black he saw as he walked to stand behind the only seat. There was the standard console and keyboard too, and he knew that if any room in the palace had AI access, this one sure did.

Helena pulled out the chair and had him sit. She said quite politely to AI, "This is the Duke d'Avigdor. Validate him and then follow his commands."

He grinned at her. "I couldn't have even gotten into the room if AI didn't know who I was," he said.

She nodded. "I will go—you can do up your mission from here, and then let me know later how it all worked out. Or maybe the aliens walking down the palace hallways will," she said with a bit of humor.

He nodded and a faint smile followed her out of the room as she closed the door behind her.

"Time," he said, and he instructed AI to follow his directions. "Screens across the top, all showing views of the alien intruder ship of Ghayth. I want to see all the ships there in wide display."

Immediately, the seven ships surrounding the intruder ship came on-screen, along with the *Wilson*, the Ghayth space station.

First were the *Coventry* and *Crimson I*, then *the Crimson II* and the *Whitney*, and then the *Newton* and the *Crimson III*. In front of the *Wilson* sat the *Defiant* with Captain Magnusson and the marines.

"We're in place," he said to himself.

It had taken a whole bunch of favors to get to this

point. It had taken several EYES ONLY from various friends here on the RIM to not be there in person.

Admiral McQueen had stated that he'd pull the three RIM Navy ships if the duke was present in person. No equivocations and no excuses.

Admiral Higgins had shouted the same thing at him, totally disregarding any kind of respect for a Royal. He'd resign as soon as he heard that the duke showed up.

The Baroness had said, as nicely as possible, that perhaps the *Defiant* might need to come back to Neres for service and take the marines with it.

And lastly, his wife. Helena had listened to him rant and rave about being hogtied—even though he was now a duke—and not being right there in the middle of the upcoming mission. She had nodded. She had waited for him to finish.

He recalled her words from last night. *"I agree with your friends. Do NOT even think of going. Do it from here. That is, sit with all the controls right here at hand and manage the firefight—if there is one—from here."* She had turned then to leave him alone, and he had just stared at her as she had left their salon.

Last night, he had stood there and tried to come up with a reason why he had to be with the others above Ghayth. There were none.

He sagged. Today, he was going to, for the first

time, miss the action on a personal level.

"Duke's job ..." he said to himself, and now as he sat in the war room at the helm of the mission, he knew they were all right. He had to rise to the position and this was a part of it.

He looked at the second row of displays and said, "AI, put the seven captains on the screen for me, and notify them that I'm here and it's T-minus five minutes so that they can notify their crews and the marines."

The faces of his task force captains appeared, and they all checked in.

"Put Bram on-screen as well, please."

Bram's face appeared and he grinned at his duke. "All quiet here on the *Wilson*, Your Grace. And I get not a single stray thought from the Praix. Master Adepts they may well be, but nada from them so far," he said, and he grinned back at Tanner.

Seven captains, Bram, and one more to add, Tanner thought. "AI, also put Major Stal up there too, please, you'll find him on the *Defiant*."

Alver's smile appeared in moments and he fully saluted his Task Force commander. "Ready, willing, and able," he said.

"Must ask, Alver, what caliber did they find for you?"

"The .454 Casull—ain't been made in five

centuries, and she's got huge stopping power. Them alien birds are big ones, so we figure we're fine, Your Grace," he said and smiled.

"AI, I want to see platoon leaders too—not them but their body cams—on display, and show via captions where they are so I know," he said. And moments later, six new displays appeared below the bank holding Alver. The marine body cams showed quiet calm marines sitting in their cargo bay. All lined up and seated. All ready to be commanded. All ready for whatever was to come.

Tanner looked at the countdown. One minute forty seconds left. He noted the positions and gave his war room AI instructions about what to show and follow at zero time.

He looked back again at the display of the ships around the Praix and watched the time count down. At exactly zero, he keyed in to talk to the seven captains and gave them the orders they knew were coming.

"This is task force commander, Duke d'Avigdor. You are all go for Stage One—engage the enemy," he said firmly.

He'd planned this down to the minute. He had no idea if this would work. There were dominoes that needed to fall, and knock over others—or else the whole alien intruder mission was moot.

When the captains received the engage signal, the

first six ships began to move. The three RIM Navy ships all began to move away from the Praix ship. Slowly, and in sync, the *Coventry*, the *Newton*, and the *Whitney* moved back and back even more. The Praix ship sent out a quick ultra-bright teal ray that quickly locked on the three ships as they began to move, and then the ray disappeared.

The aliens knew that the RIM Navy ships were underway. The three Caliphate ships, instead of moving back, drew in closer to the intruder ship. They came within ten miles of the Praix ship, then eight miles, as Tanner noted on his screens sidebar. No ultra-bright teal ray shone out from the Praix ship.

Now the Caliphate ships were six miles away. No ultra-bright teal ray came from the Praix ship.

The Caliphate ships closed to five miles with the force field just a mile ahead, and still no ultra-bright teal ray.

At four miles away, the ships were about to touch the force field. Tanner knew this was the crux of the whole mission. The *Crimson I* and *Crimson II* stopped at just less than four miles from the Praix ship, but the *Crimson III* went on. Still, no ultra-bright teal ray emitted from the intruder ship.

At the edge of the force field, nothing happened, and Tanner could breathe again. The *Crimson III* went on closer and closer until it stopped just off the huge disk that sat in the center of the mile-long Praix intruder ship.

It now lay within the alien force field. The red metal Xithricite hull plating made the ship invisible to the Praix technology. They couldn't see it. And their force fields therefore could not stop the ships.

Tanner made a quick comment to the war room AI to have him give the possibility of Xithricite missiles a looksee later.

As the *Crimson III* nestled into the area just beside the wide-open Praix ship landing bay, Tanner once again went back to his captains.

"As you can see, we're in. No force field can stop a red metal ship. So, it's time for our marines," he said.

"Captain Magnusson. Go to Stage Two, Captain —and once on target, hold that position for your marines no matter what."

The *Defiant* moved off from its mission start location, in front of the *Wilson*, to arrow right in at speed toward that landing bay on the Praix ship.

It, like the Caliphate Xithricite-clad ships, passed right through the force field, and the Praix didn't even notice.

At the landing bay, the *Defiant* jockeyed a bit to swing first to port to avoid something, and then it set down inside the landing bay. The relay from the *Defiant* began screaming with klaxons blaring and lights flashing.

"They know we're knocking now ..." Alver said, and he and his marines poured down the landing ramp of the *Defiant*. The camera switched to show his body cam along with the body cams of his platoon leaders as they ran down the ramp before the *Defiant* had even set down on its shuttle landing tripods.

The Praix captain was busy up in the atrium, gliding and enjoying the streams around him that helped him think he was flying over one of his favorite planets—the one with the bright green foliage and the smaller pink tall, tall palms. He wished he could just fly here forever, but alas not so much more than five minutes later, he received a mind message from the engineering flock leader.

"Something is going on down in the big landing bay. Something has landed therein and the ship's AI is screaming with security cautions."

"Impossible," he said to himself. "Nothing can get through the *Wisp's* force field. Nothing. Nothing could actually land in the *Wisp's* landing bay."

As he fluttered out of the direct flow of air to descend, he sent out a mind reach to the landing bay area, looking for whatever was there.

There was no registration of any kind of intruder. There was no measure—that he could find—of anyone there.

"Stupid AI," he said to himself.

He sent out a mind message to the security flock leader. *Seems she was here somewhere in the atrium, maybe still way up there,* he thought. He passed along his own directions to her. *"Go to the landing bay. Take some security officers, and when the situation has been looked at, let him know."*

Easy and on point, he thought. *Now ... back to those beautiful pink palms ...*

Alver took point inside the starboard side of the landing bay that was almost four hundred feet wide, and he noted the two platoon leaders were properly positioned. One platoon had split and half stood here beside him while the other half was over on the far side. Both groups were plastered against the interior walls of the bay, outward from the two very tall corridors with their wide, fifty-foot high doorways. The remaining platoon was picketed around the *Defiant*, the only craft in the bay.

"No other ships, noted. No one here also, noted. No evidence of any kind of unloading or loading equipment either. And from here inside, we see that the bay also has the same kind of force field that was used to protect the ship itself. Hence," Alver added, "it was no problem with the *Defiant* entering the ship. They just do not see us. But as those klaxons are still wailing, they know something is up down here. We await their entry, Duke," he finished off.

Tanner grunted. Yes, blaring klaxons meant someone was on their way.

He sent his last message to Alver. "Caution, Major ... and stay on Stage Three!"

Alver must have agreed, as an okay sign done with his left hand was jammed in front of his body cam.

Moments later, Tanner heard Alver's commands to the two platoons.

"Troops, power belts on. Safeties off on your sidearms. Meet all aliens with respect, but remember, rules of engagement state that we are here to enforce the RIM Confederacy Constitution. Meet force with force, and we want no casualties— on our side at least," he finished off. With a big grin, he yelled out, "Oorah, marines," and all of the marines in the landing bay yelled it back.

And they waited.

By the countdown timer on his console, it took more than twenty minutes of the klaxons blaring for anything to happen in the landing bay.

Alver first saw the Praix appear across the bay.

Five of them were flying but with little wing action, he noted. A huge influx of air rushing into the bay accompanied them.

Yes, they were tall, and yes, they were what he'd have to call ugly too. They had bald heads and feathers that were shiny but looked somehow like tired leaves on a plant that needed water. They had what he'd call some kind of forearm and digits that he supposed they used when they needed to manually do things. The feet, which were big and heavily scaled, had talons that were six inches long. But their heads—with no feathered foliage—were big. Those heads held brains he was sure were probably the base of all their powers.

He watched carefully as the five of them looked down from a hundred feet up, and they hovered there for a full minute.

"Sending out news, I'd bet," Tanner said, "of intruders on board."

The klaxons ended. The lights stopped flashing, and yet the Praix hung there above the marines and the *Defiant*.

Alver grinned and stepped forward, marching toward the center of the space below them, and waved up at the Praix. After waving to them, he just stood there, looking up. "First contact," he said to himself. At least he was trying.

While no one was ever sure, the Praix above

them may have gotten a message from elsewhere on the ship, but for some reason, the five alighted just twenty feet from Alver, their wings folding up neatly as their talons folded up as well and they faced him. Their faces, Tanner could see, passed along no evidence of any kind of emotion or meaning or any kind of communication.

Alver nodded to them and said, "We hate to have invited ourselves in, but we are from the RIM Confederacy, and your ship is in our space. So we need to know—what is it you desire?"

The Praix just looked at him. There was again no facial changes. Their beaks did look a bit tucked in, Tanner thought.

"I get a read now," Bram said from aboard the *Wilson*. "They're just sending back what they see—us—to their captain, I think—if the word is captain."

Tanner nodded. *Makes sense,* he thought.

The Praix stood and just watched, as Bram added more. "There appears to be a huge backlash going on—from the little that I can see—the Praix in the bay are not being believed by the rest of them on the ship—oh, I see exactly seventy-one minds. No more or less," he added.

Seventy-one against billions ... should be an easy one, eh? Tanner thought.

The Praix in the middle of the five in front of

Alver took three steps toward the marine and stopped. He appeared to be trying to make some kind of communication, but that was not to be, as a shot rang out.

Captain Magnusson yelled, "Got him, Alver" and moved toward the Praix who was now writhing on the landing bay deck. Magnusson had obviously snuck out of the *Defiant*, and he had closed the distance to be within thirty feet of the grouping.

"Shit," Alver said, and then he yelled, "Medic" and moved toward the downed alien, to try to help.

"Shit," Tanner said, copying Alver. "Task force, be ready for anything."

At that point, thirty more Praix suddenly flew into the landing bay, and all hell broke loose.

"Well, shit," Bram added. "They want revenge, Duke," he said suddenly.

As the new group split in two, from well above, some kind of a laser shone down on the marines who'd taken what little cover there was. As the Praix lasers hit the marines, the power belts protected them. The return fire from the marines was loud and swift.

The .454 Casulls spoke out loud, and each time a marine shot, a Praix fell from the sky. In less than a minute, the landing bay deck took another corpse, and they were all dead except for the original one

287

hit by Magnusson.

Tanner was fit to be tied. "Alver, take Captain Magnusson into custody, he'll face a court martial for this. Check your men and their power belts. There's still about the same number of Praix on that ship. We'll want to find them, round them up—"

"Your Grace—the whole ship knows what just happened. The Praix, like we Issians, use mind reading to talk to each other. They know that every single one here—except for the one that Magnusson shot—is dead. They have no sense of real regret, but they also reach consensus in moments—all linked like that," he said.

He gripped his brow for a second and then looked at his duke. "They are all coming to the bay —but from what I see, they are prepared to capitulate. They are walking—this is a sign that they have surrendered, I take it, so this might take a moment. May I go over to help with that, Duke?"

Tanner nodded and instructed the captain of the *Crimson I* to go back to the *Wilson*, pick up Bram, and take him directly to the Praix ship. That took almost ten minutes, and when Bram arrived, he waited as they all did for the Praix to show up.

And they did. Walking, and in single file, they entered the landing bay and formed up in rows, a few more than thirty of them.

One Praix took the lead position, and he turned

to Bram to make his needs known. As he communicated via mind message, Bram spoke the message out loud.

"We, the Praix, bow to your superior technology. You are our masters. You also have already enslaved the Issians, we now learn. We will do as you please." The Praix opened his wings and did what some thought later was a Praix bow of surrender.

Bram nodded to the Praix, and everyone waited for the task force commander to speak.

"Thank the Praix. Remind him of what happened here and how it was not our wish to begin our relationship in this manner. That we will hold our own officer, who took this action upon himself, accountable for the loss of the Praix who lie here today. Thank him for their patience, having arrived months ago, and awaiting the decision from the Issians. And lastly, we offer them to follow their own traditions to allow them to handle their dead in their own manner."

He sat back and watched as Bram turned to the Praix captain and transferred his message. He watched for more than three more hours as Alver and his marines mopped up. They carefully moved the Praix dead to a room off the bay, where they were instantly frozen and preserved for later traditional cremation, which the Praix had told

Bram.

He signed off on the suggestion from Bram to ask the Master Adept to put together a team of Issians to come to Ghayth to handle the Praix problem. He was the one who'd asked Bram—and Bram had just whistled with his awe at trying to work out all the details of the integration of these aliens into the RIM Confederacy ... at least that's how he saw it.

Duke.

New Duke.

New aliens.

New victims.

New traitorous captain.

New just about everything, he thought as he slipped into bed beside Helena and spooned her.

He dropped an arm over her waist and got comfortable, but as usual, sleep was a long way off.

On Eons, the Master Adept updated the Praix book and smiled as she finished her entry. She had noted that all had gone according to her plans ...

Only an hour before the task force incursion, the Praix had learned that the Issians were going to turn down their offer—their orders—to re-join the Praix.

The captain, who had fired that shot, had

received a full mental push from the combined inner circle, and he had rushed out of the *Defiant* full of hate and had shot the Praix. He would have no idea as to why he had done so.

The Praix captain, she had seen via Bram, had spoken the truth. They were prepared to be somehow absorbed into the RIM Confederacy.

That did worry her somewhat. What little she knew of the Praix was that they accepted defeat poorly—they'd never had a loss at the hands of another race. So, this easy capitulation might be hiding some other backstory she'd not yet learned.

Bram had unknowingly told the duke that the Praix problem needed full Issian help, and she expected that message to come later tomorrow in the morning here on Eons.

Now with dawn only hours away, she left her private study to go out into her general quarters. At the window, she looked out at the blackness beyond the galaxy. At this time of year, Eons lay on the outer side of its orbit around its blue sun; the only real things to see were the few fuzzy dots of distant galaxies.

She looked down but the darkness was thick on the farms beyond the walled city. She couldn't see the one that was for sale, but she still knew it was down there. Now, she'd noted, there was another too that had a for sale sign on it, and that was a

291

good sign.

"Not as good as having the Praix to manage—on behalf of the RIM for sure, but still ... there were generations to have repayment for, weren't there?" she said to herself as she looked up at the ringed moon above her. "Perhaps it's time for the Issians to find their destiny ..."

Epilogue ~

The man who had been Captain Magnusson rolled over on the hard steel bench in his cell, and he tried once again to find sleep as an escape.

That wasn't going to work, and he had known for a while that it didn't work.

Last night he'd tossed and turned and had tried to find a way to lie on his steel bed with some degree—any degree—of comfort.

He had found none for hours.

His mind was the problem, he knew.

He'd done something on the Praix ship that he found was so alien to him that it couldn't be true.

He had crept out of the *Defiant*, a Colt in his hand that he had taken from a crewman. He had walked up to where Major Stal was facing off against the Praix—who had then taken some steps toward the marine. And he had charged in and shot the Praix.

Luckily, the Praix had lived, but it was touch and go for a few days, he'd learned.

But the shooting itself?

He had no idea why.

He had no idea what for.

In fact, he doubted it had been him.

It was as if it was someone else and it'd been an out-of-body experience.

He lay still with the slow throb of his pulse in his

ear as he had his arm tucked under his head. He slid a leg down farther and that didn't help either. So he got up and did fifty sit-ups and twenty push-ups. He lay down, barely winded, and hoped that this might help him get tired and help him fall off to sleep quicker.

He wanted to know more. He needed to know more. He had tried to get to see the duke to ask for help, but that had been refused. He had tried to get to see his Baroness, but again, he was refused. He had tried to see Bram to see if he knew or could help and was refused.

Instead, he sat in the brig here in the city jail on Neres. He faced court martial in a few weeks, they'd said. And because it was an attempted murder charge, he wouldn't even get a bail hearing for a week more he'd been told.

He lay there and nursed the thought that it could have been someone else ... but that he knew was not true.

The only thing that he knew was true was that an innocent man was about to be tried ...

BOOK THIRTEEN OF THE RIM CONFEDERACY

Inwards Bound

Prologue ~

Bram tossed on his bunk and thought about the current state of affairs in his life.

He should have perhaps thought about his station as an ex-Adept Officer in the Barony navy.

Also ex-Barony navy too.

Now a plain lieutenant commander in the Duchy navy.

He swept a foot and most of a leg from underneath the covers and sighed.

He was going, he knew to amount to something, but what exactly?

His life so far had been—well until the duke came along at least, pretty uneventful.

He had grown up on Eons, his parents had been Issians but had chosen to be merchants instead of working within the cult, for a reason he'd never gotten. He'd asked, he remembered but that was met with a shake of the head and silence.

He knew that many many Issians, millions in fact on Eons had little to do with the faith—but he had gravitated towards being a faithful member since about grade school. Since he'd seen vids of what it was like to be in the navy as a real live spaceman. Recruiting vids that they were for sure, but at graduation from his high school, he applied and

was accepted at the RIM Confederacy Naval
Academy, just outside of Dessau.

He'd realized too, that upon graduation, he
would most likely be asked to swear to the faith
that he would be true to Eons first, and the navy
second. That was what was expected by the inner
circle—the ones that ran the faith on Eons.

And on the RIM too.

He graduated, and while he was in the middle of
the class as he'd excelled at little, he had at least
passed and had sworn his to his faith too.

His first posting, was on the RN Marwick as
their new Adept Officer under the brand new
captain Scott.

Now his friend and mentor at the time he was
scary. He'd fought those pirates those long years
ago and had done well enough to earn a field
promotion from lieutenant to captain, up two whole
ranks.

The days of being on the Marwick brought mixed
emotions to Bram as he rolled over onto his left side
and faced the bulkhead just a half an arm's length
away.

He shied away from other memories and pushed
them back, rather than re-live the hurt and pain of
death and duty for many. The whole prison riot
and his agreeing to resign from the RIM navy and
join his captain over in the Barony navy was also

something he was not going to re-live either.

He sat up and tucked the extra pillow behind his head and sighed.

No sleep truck had even gone by for him to grab onto and slide into and he kept the thought of Gia away.

He would like to see her and he knew that he could do that but he resisted.

That would be something to hold out for, he thought as he scrunched that extra pillow a bit to ease down a little on the bed.

Gym tomorrow in the early part of the morning, he grinned at himself.

He was getting paunchy and maybe a hundred core crunches would help a bit.

Hurt a bit for sure, he said to himself as he closed his eyes once more...trying to find sleep....

Available in the winter of 2016!

Want to get early notice when we've got a new RIM Confederacy Series book launch?

Just drop by www.jimrudnick.ca and leave you email address and we'll let you know!

Or drop by our Face Book page at www.facebook.com/theRIMConfederacy/

The RIM CONFEDERACY: Captured Aliens

Dear Reader...

If you've made it this far, you're most likely thinking that this was the best SciFi you've ever read. Or maybe not.

Maybe Tanner Scott wasn't your cup of tea?

Or you hate the Baroness and her scheming ways?

Or does the Caliph look like an upcoming tyrant?

So I'd like to ask you for a favor? Would you mind taking a few minutes to write a review for me please?

And I'm talking honest too! Nothing makes us writers get better than book reviews!

Your comments help others know what to expect when they're looking for a great SciFi read...

And thanks once again, I'm looking forward to reading your comments!

Jim Rudnick
2016